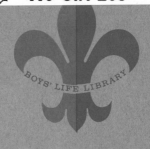

BOYS' LIFE LIBRARY

The Boys' Life Book of
Outer Space Stories

For several generations, millions of boys all over America have been reading BOYS' LIFE magazine, the official publication of the Boy Scouts of America. Now from the pages of this popular magazine BOYS' LIFE LIBRARY presents ten tales to intrigue and delight young science-fiction fans.

THE
BOYS' LIFE
BOOK
OF
OUTER SPACE
STORIES

Selected by the Editors of *Boys' Life*

Illustrations by Harry Kane

Random House   New York

Acknowledgments

The publishers wish to thank the following for permission to use these stories, all of which have appeared in *Boys' Life* magazine, copyright 1956, 1957, 1959, 1960, 1961, 1963, by Boy Scouts of America: Larry Sternig for A NEW GAME, by A. M. Lightner; William F. Hallstead for SPACE LANE CADET; Edward W. Wood for LOAD OF TROUBLE; Harold Matson Company for THE MAN, by Ray Bradbury, copyright 1948 by Standard Magazines, Inc., originally published in Thrilling Wonder Stories, Feb., 1949; Larry Sternig for BEST FRIEND, by A. M. Lightner; James V. Hinrichs for THE TERRIBLE INTRUDERS; Richard J. Harper for THE SAMARITAN; William W. Greer for QUADS FROM VARS; Gene L. Henderson for TIGER BY THE TAIL; Lurton Blassingame for THE SMALLEST MOON, by Don Wilcox.

Library of Congress catalog card number: 63-9626

2 964

CONTENTS

The Boys' Life Book of
Outer Space Stories

THE
MAN

by Ray Bradbury

Captain Hart stood in the door of the rocket. "Why don't they come?" he asked.

"Who knows?" said Martin, his lieutenant. "Do I know, Captain?"

"What kind of a place is this, anyway?" The captain lighted a cigar. He tossed the match out into the glittering meadow. The grass started to burn.

Martin moved to stamp it out with his boot.

"No," ordered Captain Hart, "let it burn. Maybe they'll come see what's happening then, the ignorant fools."

Martin shrugged and withdrew his foot from the spreading fire.

Captain Hart examined his watch. "An hour

ago we landed here, and does the welcoming com-
mittee rush out with a brass band to shake our
hands? No indeed! Here we ride millions of miles
through space and the fine citizens of some silly
town on some unknown planet ignore us!" He
snorted, tapping his watch. "Well, I'll just give
them five more minutes, and then—"

"And then what?" asked Martin, ever so
politely, watching the captain's jowls shake.

"We'll fly over their city again and give them
a good scare." His voice grew quieter. "Do you
think, Martin, maybe they didn't see us land?"

"They saw us. They looked up as we flew
over."

"Then why aren't they running across the
field? Are they hiding? Are they yellow?"

Martin shook his head. "No. Take these binoculars, sir. See for yourself. Everbody's walking
around. They're not frightened. They—well, they
just don't seem to care."

Captain Hart placed the binoculars to his tired
eyes. Martin looked up and had time to observe
the lines and the grooves of irritation, tiredness,
nervousness there. Hart looked a million years
old; he never slept, he ate little, and drove himself
on, on. Now his mouth moved under the held
binoculars, his voice came sharply.

"Really, Martin, I don't know why we bother. We build rockets, we go to all the trouble of crossing space, searching for them, and this is what we get. Neglect. Look at those idiots wander about in there. Don't they realize how big this is? The first space flight to touch their provincial land. How many times does that happen? Are they that blasé?"

Martin didn't know.

Captain Hart gave him back the binoculars wearily. "Why do we do it, Martin? This space travel, I mean. Always on the go. Always searching. Our insides always tight, never any rest."

"Maybe we're looking for peace and quiet. Certainly there's none on Earth," said Martin.

"No, there's not, is there?" Captain Hart was thoughtful, the fire damped down. "You think maybe that's why we're going out to the stars, eh, Martin? Looking for our lost souls, is that it? Trying to get away from our evil planet to a good one?"

"Perhaps, sir. Certainly we're looking for something."

Captain Hart cleared his throat and tightened back into sharpness. "Well, right now we're looking for the mayor of that city. Run in, tell them who we are, the first rocket expedition to Planet

Forty-three in Star System Three. Captain Hart sends his salutations and desires to meet the mayor. On the double!"

"Yes, sir." Martin walked slowly across the meadow.

"Hurry!" snapped the captain.

"Yes, sir!" Martin trotted away. Then he walked again, smiling to himself.

The captain had smoked two cigars before Martin returned. Martin stopped and looked up into the door of the rocket, swaying, seemingly unable to focus his eyes or think.

"Well?" snapped Hart. "What happened? Are they coming to welcome us?"

"No." Martin had to lean dizzily against the ship.

"Why not?"

"It's not important," said Martin. He was looking at the golden city and blinking.

"Say something!" cried the captain. "Aren't they interested in our rocket?"

Martin said, "What? Oh. The rocket? No, they're not interested. Seems we came at an inopportune time."

"Inopportune time!"

Martin was patient. "Captain, listen. Something big happened yesterday in that city. It's so big, so important that we're second-rate—second fiddle. I've got to sit down." He lost his balance and sat heavily, gasping for air.

The captain chewed his cigar angrily. "What happened?"

Martin lifted his head slowly. "Sir, yesterday, in that city, a remarkable man appeared—good, intelligent, compassionate, and infinitely wise!"

The captain glared at his lieutenant. "What's that to do with us?"

"It's hard to explain. But he was a man for whom they'd waited a long time—a million years maybe. And yesterday he walked into their city. That's why today, sir, our rocket landing means nothing."

The captain sat down violently. "Who was it? Not Ashley? He didn't arrive in his rocket before us and steal my glory, did he?" He seized Martin's arm. His face was pale and dismayed.

"Not Ashley, sir."

"Then it was Burton! I knew it. Burton stole in ahead of us and ruined my landing! You can't trust anyone any more."

"Not Burton, either, sir," said Martin quietly.

The captain was incredulous. "There were only three rockets. We were in the lead. This man who got here ahead of us? What was his name!"

"He didn't have a name. He doesn't need one. It would be different on every planet, sir."

The captain stared at his lieutenant with hard, cynical eyes.

"Well, what did he do that was so wonderful that nobody even looks at our ship?"

"For one thing," said Martin steadily, "he healed the sick and comforted the poor. He fought hypocrisy and dirty politics and sat among the people, talking, through the day."

"Is that so wonderful?"

"Yes, Captain."

"I don't get this." The captain confronted Martin, peered into his face and eyes. "You been drinking, eh?" He was suspicious. He backed away. "I don't understand."

Martin looked at the city. "Captain, if you don't understand, there's no way of telling you."

The captain followed his gaze. The city was quiet and beautiful and a great peace lay over it. The captain stepped forward, taking his cigar from his lips. He squinted first at Martin, then at the golden spires of the buildings.

"You don't mean—you can't mean—That man you're talking about couldn't be—"

Martin nodded. "That's what I mean, sir."

The captain stood silently, not moving. He drew himself up.

"I don't believe it," he said at last.

At high noon Captain Hart walked briskly into

the city, accompanied by Lieutenant Martin and an assistant who was carrying some electrical equipment. Every once in a while the captain laughed loudly, put his hands on his hips and shook his head.

The mayor of the town confronted him. Martin set up a tripod, screwed a box onto it, and switched on the batteries.

"Are you the mayor?" The captain jabbed a finger out.

"I am," said the mayor.

The delicate apparatus stood between them, controlled and adjusted by Martin and the assistant. Instantaneous translations from any language were made by the box. The words sounded crisply on the mild air of the city.

"About this occurrence yesterday," said the captain. "It occurred?"

"It did."

"You have witnesses?"

"We have."

"May we talk to them?"

"Talk to any of us," said the mayor. "We are all witnesses."

In an aside to Martin the captain said, "Mass hallucination." To the mayor, "What did this man look like?"

"That would be hard to say," said the mayor,

smiling a little.

"Why would it?"

"Opinions might differ slightly."

"I'd like your opinion, sir, anyway," said the captain. "Record this," he snapped to Martin over his shoulder. The lieutenant pressed the button of a hand recorder.

"Well," said the mayor of the city, "he was a very gentle and kind man. He was of a great and knowing intelligence."

"Yes—yes, I know, I know." The captain waved his fingers. "Generalizations. I want something specific. What did he look like?"

"I don't believe that is important," replied the mayor.

The captain snapped his fingers. "There was something or other—a healing?"

"Many healings," said the mayor.

"May I see one?"

"You may," said the mayor. "My son." He nodded at a small boy who stepped forward. "He was afflicted with a withered arm. Now, look upon it."

At this the captain laughed tolerantly. "Yes, yes. This isn't even circumstantial evidence, you know. I didn't see the boy's withered arm. I see only his arm whole and well. That's no proof. What proof have you that the boy's arm was withered yesterday and today is well?"

"My word is my proof," said the mayor simply.

"My dear man!" cried the captain. "You don't expect me to go on hearsay, do you? Oh no!"

"I'm sorry," said the mayor, looking upon the captain with what appeared to be curiosity and pity.

"Do you have any pictures of the boy before today?" asked the captain.

After a moment a large oil portrait was carried forth, showing the son with a withered arm.

"My dear fellow!" The captain waved it away. "Anybody can paint a picture. Paintings lie. I want a photograph of the boy."

There was no photograph. Photography was not a known art in their society.

"Well," sighed the captain, face twitching, "let me talk to a few other citizens. We're getting nowhere." He pointed at a woman. "You." She hesitated. "Yes, you, come here," ordered the captain. "Tell me about this man you saw."

The woman looked steadily at the captain. "He walked among us and was very fine and good."

"What color were his eyes?"

"The color of the sun, the color of the sea, the color of a flower, the color of the mountains, the color of the night."

"That'll do." The captain threw up his hands. "See, Martin? Absolutely nothing. Some charlatan wanders through whispering sweet nothings in their ears and—"

"Please, stop it," said Martin.

The captain stepped back. "What?"

"You heard what I said," said Martin. "I like these people. I believe what they say. You're entitled to your opinion, but keep it to yourself, sir."

"You can't talk to me this way," shouted the captain.

"I've had enough of your high-handedness," replied Martin. "Leave these people alone. They've got something good and decent, and you come and foul up the nest and sneer at it. Well, I've talked to them too. I've gone through the city and seen their faces, and they've got something you'll never have—a little simple faith, and they'll move mountains with it. You, you're boiled because someone stole your act, got here ahead of you and made you unimportant!"

"I'll give you five seconds to finish," remarked the captain. "I understand. You've been under a strain, Martin. Months of traveling in space, nostalgia, loneliness. And now, with this thing happening, I sympathize, Martin. I overlook your petty insubordination."

"I don't overlook your petty tyranny," replied Martin. "I'm stepping out. I'm staying here."

"You can't do that!"

"Can't I? Try and stop me. This is what I came looking for. I didn't know it, but this is it. This is for me. Take your filth somewhere else and foul up other nests with your doubt and your—scientific method!" He looked swiftly about. "These people have had an experience, and you can't seem to get it through your head that it's really happened and we were lucky enough almost to be in on it.

"People on Earth have talked about this man for centuries after he walked through the old world. We've all wanted to see him and hear him and never had the chance. And now, today, we just missed seeing him by a few hours."

Captain Hart looked at Martin's cheeks. "You're crying like a baby. Stop it."

"I don't care."

"Well, I do. In front of these natives we're to keep up a front. You're overwrought. As I said, I forgive you."

"I don't want your forgiveness."

"You idiot. Can't you see this is one of Burton's tricks, to fool these people, to bilk them, to establish his oil and mineral concerns under a religious guise! You fool, Martin. You absolute fool! You

should know Earthmen by now. They'll do anything—lie, cheat, steal, kill, to get their ends. Anything is fine if it works; the true pragmatist, that's
Burton. You know him!"

The captain scoffed heavily. "Come off it,
Martin, admit it; this is the sort of scaly thing
Burton might carry off, polish up these citizens
and pluck them when they're ripe."

"No," said Martin, thinking of it.

The captain put his hand up. "That's Burton.
That's him. That's his dirt, that's his criminal
way. I have to admire the old dragon. Flaming in
here in a blaze and a halo and a soft word and a
loving touch, with a medicated salve here and a
healing ray there. That's Burton all right!"

"No." Martin's voice was dazed. He covered
his eyes. "No, I won't believe it."

"You don't want to believe." Captain Hart
kept at it. "Admit it now. Admit it! It's just the
thing Burton would do. Stop daydreaming, Martin. Wake up! It's morning. This is a real world
and we're real, dirty people—Burton the dirtiest
of us all!"

Martin turned away.

"There, there, Martin," said Hart, mechani-
cally patting the man's back. "I understand.
Quite a shock for you. I know. A rotten shame,

and all that. That Burton is a rascal. You go take it easy. Let me handle this."

Martin walked off slowly toward the rocket.

Captain Hart watched him go. Then, taking a deep breath, he turned to the woman he had been questioning. "Well. Tell me some more about this man. As you were saying, madam?"

Later the officers of the rocket ship ate supper on card tables outside. The captain correlated his data to a silent Martin who sat red-eyed, brooding over his meal.

"Interviewed three dozen people, all of them full of the same milk and hogwash," said the captain. "It's Burton's work all right, I'm positive. He'll be spilling back in here tomorrow or next week to consolidate his miracles and beat us out in our contracts. I think I'll stick on and spoil it for him."

Martin glanced up sullenly. "I'll kill him," he said.

"Now, now, Martin! There, there, boy."

"I'll kill him—so help me, I will."

"We'll put an anchor on his wagon. You have to admit he's clever. Unethical but clever."

"He's dirty."

"You must promise not to do anything violent."

Captain Hart checked his figures. "According to this, there were thirty miracles of healing performed, a blind man restored to vision, a leper cured. Oh, Burton's efficient, give him that."

A gong sounded. A moment later a man ran up. "Captain, sir. A report! Burton's ship is coming down. Also the Ashley ship, sir!"

"See!" Captain Hart beat the table. "Here come the jackals to the harvest! They can't wait to feed. Wait till I confront them. I'll make them cut me in on this feat—I will!"

Martin looked sick. He stared at the captain.

"Business, my dear boy, business," said the captain.

Everybody looked up. Two rockets swung down out of the sky. When the rockets landed they almost crashed.

"What's wrong with those fools?" cried the captain, jumping up. The men ran across the meadowlands to the steaming ships. The captain arrived. The air-lock door popped open on Burton's ship. A man fell out into their arms.

"What's wrong?" cried Captain Hart.

The man lay on the ground. They bent over him. He was burned, badly burned. His body was covered with wounds and scars and tissue that was inflamed and smoking. He looked up out of

puffed eyes and his thick tongue moved in his
split lips.

"What happened?" demanded the captain,
kneeling down, shaking the man's arm.

"Sir, sir," whispered the dying man. "Forty-
eight hours ago, back in Space Sector Seventy-
nine DFS, off Planet One in this system, our ship
and Ashley's ship ran into a cosmic storm, sir."
Liquid ran gray from the man's nostrils. Blood
trickled from his mouth. "Wiped out. All crew.
Burton dead. Ashley died an hour ago. Only three
survivors."

"Listen to me!" shouted Hart, bending over
the bleeding man. "You didn't come to this
planet before this very hour?"

Silence.

"Answer me!" cried Hart.

The dying man said, "No. Storm. Burton dead
two days ago. This first landing on any world in
six months."

"Are you sure?" shouted Hart, shaking violently, gripping the man in his hands. "Are you
sure?"

"Sure, sure," mouthed the dying man.

"Burton died two days ago? You're positive?"

"Yes, yes," whispered the man. His head fell
forward. The man was dead.

The captain knelt beside the silent body. The captain's face twitched, the muscles jerking involuntarily. The other members of the crew stood back of him looking down. Martin waited. The captain asked to be helped to his feet, finally, and this was done. They stood looking at the city. "That means—"

"That means?" said Martin.

"We're the only ones who've been here," whispered Captain Hart. "And that man—"

"What about that man, Captain?" asked Martin.

The captain's face twitched senselessly. He looked very old indeed, and gray. His eyes were glazed. He moved forward.

"Come along, Martin. Come along. Hold me up; for my sake, hold me. I'm afraid I'll fall. And hurry. We can't waste time—"

They moved, stumbling, toward the city, in the long dry grass, in the blowing wind.

Several hours later they were sitting in the mayor's auditorium. A thousand people had come and talked and gone. The captain had remained seated, his face haggard, listening, listening. There was so much light in the faces of those who came and testified and talked he could not bear to see them. And all the while his hands traveled, on his knees, together; on his belt, jerking and quivering.

When it was over, Captain Hart turned to the mayor and with strange eyes said: "But you must know where he went?"

"He didn't say where he was going," replied the mayor.

"To one of the other nearby worlds?" demanded the captain.

"I don't know."

"You must know."

"Do you see him?" asked the mayor, indicating the crowd.

The captain looked. "No."

"Then he is probably gone," said the mayor.

"Probably, probably!" cried the captain weakly. "I've made a horrible mistake, and I want to see him now. Why, it just came to me, this is a most unusual thing in history. To be in on something like this. Why, the chances are one in billions we'd arrive at one certain planet among millions of planets the day after he came! You must know where he's gone!"

"Each finds him in his own way," replied the mayor gently.

"You're hiding him." The captain's face grew slowly ugly. Some of the old hardness returned in stages. He began to stand up.

"No," said the mayor.

"You know where he is then?" The captain's fingers twitched at the leather holster on his right side.

"I couldn't tell you where he is, exactly," said the mayor.

"I advise you to start talking."

"There's no way," said the mayor, "to tell you anything."

"Liar!" The captain took out a small steel gun. An expression of pity came into the mayor's face as he looked at Hart.

"You're very tired," he said. "You've traveled a long way and you belong to a tired people who've been without faith a long time, and you want to believe so much now that you're interfering with yourself. You'll only make it harder if you kill. You'll never find him that way."

"Where'd he go? He told you; you know. Come on, tell me!" The captain waved the gun.

The mayor shook his head.

"Tell me! Tell me!"

The gun cracked once, twice. The mayor fell, his arm wounded.

Martin leaped forward. "Captain!"

The gun flashed at Martin. "Don't interfere."

On the floor, holding his wounded arm, the mayor looked up. "Put down your gun. You're

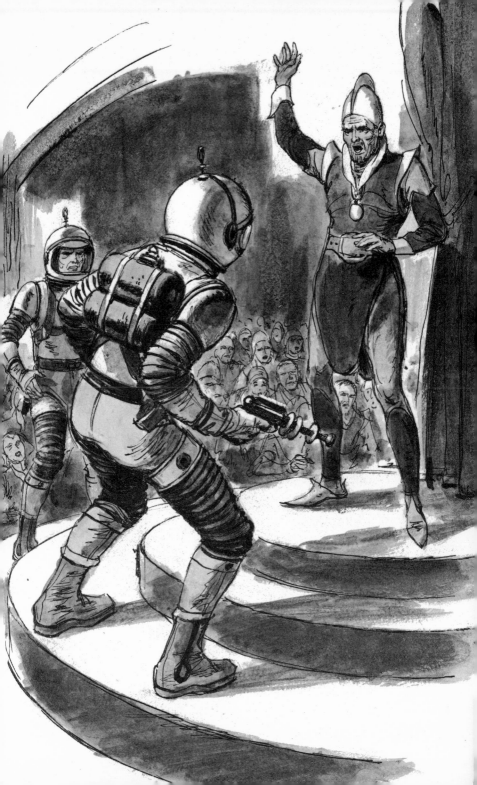

hurting yourself. You've never believed, and now that you think you believe, you hurt people because of it."

"I don't need you," said Hart, standing over him. "If I missed him by one day here, I'll go on to another world. And another and another. I'll miss him by half a day on the next planet, maybe, and a quarter of a day on the third planet, and two hours on the next, and an hour on the next, and half an hour on the next, and a minute on the next. But after that, one day I'll catch up with him! Do you hear that?" He was shouting now, leaning wearily over the man on the floor. He staggered with exhaustion. "Come along, Martin." He let the gun hang in his hand.

"No," said Martin. "I'm staying here."

"You're a fool. Stay if you like. But I'm going on, with the others, as far as I can go."

The mayor looked up at Martin. "I'll be all right. Leave me. Others will tend my wounds."

"I'll be back," said Martin. "I'll walk as far as the rocket."

They walked with vicious speed through the city. One could see with what effort the captain struggled to show all the old iron, to keep himself going. When he reached the rocket he slapped the side of it with a trembling hand. He holstered his gun. He looked at Martin.

"Well, Martin?"

Martin looked at him. "Well, Captain?"

The captain's eyes were on the sky. "Sure you won't—come with—with me, eh?"

"No, sir."

"It'll be a great adventure. I know I'll find him."

"You are set on it now, aren't you, sir?" asked Martin.

The captain's face quivered and his eyes closed. "Yes."

"There's one thing I'd like to know."

"What?"

"Sir, when you find him—if you find him," asked Martin, "what will you ask of him?"

"Why—" The captain faltered, opening his eyes. His hands clenched and unclenched. He puzzled a moment and then broke into a strange smile. "Why, I'll ask him for a little peace and quiet." He touched the rocket. "It's been a long time, a long, long time since—since I relaxed."

"Did you ever just try, Captain?"

"I don't understand," said Hart.

"Never mind. So long, Captain."

"Goodby, Martin."

The crew stood by the port. Out of their number only three were going on with Hart. Seven others were remaining behind with Martin.

Captain Hart surveyed them and uttered his verdict: "Fools!"

He, last of all, climbed into the air lock, gave a brisk salute, laughed sharply. The door slammed.

The rocket lifted into the sky on a pillar of fire. Martin watched it go far away and vanish. At the meadow's edge the mayor, supported by several men, beckoned.

"He's gone," said Martin.

"Yes, poor man, he's gone," said the mayor. "And he'll go on, planet after planet, seeking and seeking, and always and always he will be an hour late, or a half hour late, or ten minutes late, or a minute late. And finally he will miss out by only a few seconds. And when he has visited three hundred worlds and is seventy or eighty years old he will miss out by only a fraction of a second, and then a smaller fraction of a second. And he will go on and on, thinking to find that very thing which he left behind here, on this planet, in this city—"

Martin looked steadily at the mayor.

The mayor put out his hand. "Was there ever any doubt of it?" He beckoned to the others and turned. "Come along now. We mustn't keep him waiting."

They walked into the city.

A NEW GAME

by A. M. Lightner

The starship was in trouble and no one realized it more acutely than Maximilian Heyl, her pilot and captain. As he considered the best way to explain, his eyes roved from one face to another of his eight-man crew: Gene Fairless, navigator and second in command, was always reliable; and Otto Buch, the engineer, had just brought him the bad news. Henry Sands, machinist, would also grasp the situation from a hint. But when it came to Doc Bender; Harlow Downs, their geologist; and even Richard Flum, communications, you were dealing with men whose science was more abstract. They did not work directly with motors and might not understand how a starship could get into this fix. Finally, there were the two kids over by the door: Elmer Clark and Jim Berry. It was almost impossible to explain anything to kids these days, Max thought. They always knew more than you did before you began. Thank the stars, they were apprentices and didn't rate an explanation!

"The situation," he began, "is quite unprecedented. I don't want anyone to be alarmed. We've got plenty of time to hash the matter over. But Otto tells me that when we refueled back on Rigel 3, they put in a C-package instead of an X-package."

There was a puzzled silence while the men tried to interpret this information. Another man might have said it in three words: Not enough fuel. As it was, the meaning was lost on most of them—all except Henry Sands.

"The gol-darned imbecile!" he bellowed. And then as an afterthought, "It isn't possible."

"It's all too possible, Sandy," said Otto Buch. "Remember, this isn't a Class-A ship. It's a Class-C ship, reconditioned for long trips. Class-C ships were made to take the Class-C fuel package. When the X-fuel package appeared and made these longer trips possible, this ship was adjusted to take the new fuel. But it can also take the old fuel. Consequently, nobody noticed the mistake. Now if we were on one of those nice new Class-A ships . . ."

Richie Flum, the radio man spoke up. Always making a fool of himself, thought Max, except when it comes to his transistors.

"I'm sorry. I don't seem to follow this. Two kinds of fuel. We volunteered for obsolete discomforts, but nobody said anything about fuel . . ."

"Of course, they didn't," growled Sandy. "Nobody imagined this. Some idiot goofed and now we haven't enough fuel to get home! Unless we damp down the port motor . . . or shut off . . . or go into an orbit outside . . . No, it won't work. Can't you figure something, Gene?"

"I've been thinking about it ever since Otto told me," the navigator replied. "In fact, I spent two hours figuring before I dumped the problem on Max. But it's no go. We've got to get more fuel."

"That's right," Max said. "And our best bet is to go back to Rigel 3 and get the right package."

"That will make us a lot later getting home." Gene figured rapidly. "Something like six years."

The men gasped. They were to have been gone from Earth for four years. This would make it ten. Objections poured in from all sides. One man's wife had been expecting a baby when they left. He had been resigned to missing the first four years of its life, but to miss ten! Another had a girl who had vowed to wait. Ten years would be very different from four! In fact, after seven, unless communications were opened with civilization, they might all be declared legally dead and the ship lost. Their lives would hardly be worth picking up where they had been put down.

At this point a wail arose from the corner by the door.

"But . . . but . . ." lamented Elmer Clark, "this way we'll miss the Interplanetary Series!"

The laughter that greeted this statement brought a certain easing of the tension. Faced with the wreckage of their personal lives, the older men found a sports fan amusing.

"You don't understand," Jim Berry said. "We had this figured so we'd be back in time. The off-world teams only come down every five years, and to see Hayman pitch against Kandusky . . ."

"By the comet's tail!" roared Max. "I'm prepared to face the fact that we may never get home . . . that everyone's life will be disrupted . . . but now I'm supposed to worry about the great old game of baseball!"

The two boys edged out the door, only their worried faces showing, and Doc Bender undertook to restore peace.

"There's an alternative," he said. "In a short time we'll be passing the system of Aldebaran.

There's plenty of atomic material on Aldebaran 4."

The pilot and the navigator exchanged glances.

"I was waiting for someone to suggest that," Max said. "Aldebaran 4 is restricted. In case you don't know, three ships have already come to grief there. Two of them never came back."

"How do they know it was the planet?" argued Downs. "Anything could happen in space."

"It's an earth-type planet. No trouble with environment. But the natives are very hostile. It's off bounds for all exploring ships until we're ready to go there in force," said Max.

"I read the reports of the first ship. Very interesting natives from an evolutionary point of view. Some kind of highly developed reptile. I wouldn't mind a chance to look them over." Bender was the anthropologist as well as the ship's MD. His second calling was beginning to influence his thinking.

"That's just what you won't do," snapped the captain. "If we decide to put down, it will be emergency regulations. We do nothing but look for fuel. Stay close to the ship, get out as soon as possible and nobody does anything else! Understood?" He glared at each man in turn, trying to figure which one had a pet project that might foul things up. When no one answered, he decided to take a vote.

"All right then. The question to be settled is whether this is enough of an emergency to let us break the rules."

They voted unanimously in favor, and a few days later the landing was accomplished without incident. They set down in a large clearing in the midst of dense jungles. Max ordered the usual environmental tests, which seemed to check with the reports of that unfortunate earlier ship.

While the scientists were busy with this work and Richie Flum sat over his earphones, straining to pick up some intelligent message out of the alien ether, the rest of the crew crowded around the viewport. Outside lay the sinister, inscrutable land that they hoped would save them six years in space. It did not look especially different from a jungle on Earth. Perhaps a little more yellow in the green of the leaves. Perhaps a greater sprinkling of crimson flowers. Right now there was no sign that their arrival had been noted, and the wall of vegetation kept its secrets.

"We'll start prospecting at once," Max ordered, when convinced that the physical environment at least was safe. "I'll take three men. Harlow and Otto. They know what they want and how to find it. And Richie Flum. He can take the talk-box and keep us in touch. Gene will be on communications this end. He can fly the ship if necessary. If anything happens to us, Gene, get out and back to Rigel 3. And remember: stay in the ship. No exploring, no collecting, no contacting the natives!" He looked hard at Doc and swung his pack over his shoulder. "Let's go!"

Two hours later—it seemed like ten to Gene—the lieutenant was aware of Henry Sands standing in the doorway of the communications room.

"No news yet," Gene said. "Harlow thinks those hills to the north are the best bet. But the going's so rough they may not get there till evening."

"That's bad," said Sandy. "Have to spend the night."

Sandy didn't go away, and after a while Gene looked up from his listening.

"Anything on your mind, aside from this?"

"It's the kids," Sandy said. "They want to go outside."

"You know the answer to that. Nobody's to go anywhere except for the search party. And they're coming back as quick as possible."

"They're only kids. This is their first trip and they're not used to the confinement. All they want to do is throw a ball around. Exercise would be good for them."

"Where'd they get a ball?"

"Young Clark's a baseball fan. They won't be looking for specimens, as Doc would do if I turned him loose."

Gene laughed. "Clark's the one. Well, suppose you and Doc sit on the ladder and watch. You can get some sun at the same time. And Sandy, I want it clearly understood, if they knock the ball into the jungle, nobody's to go looking for it!"

Sandy lost no time in conveying the orders to the two apprentices, and with shouts of joy the boys scrambled down the ship's ladder, carrying their precious ball and bat. Doc Bender and Sandy followed more slowly and settled themselves outside the air lock.

"I don't know why I let myself be tantalized like this," complained Doc. "It's some expedition where foolish games are permitted but not serious collecting. Who knows what fascinating flora and fauna may be down there on the grass or along the edge of the jungle."

"And who knows what beastie may be waiting to snap you up," countered Sandy. "This ship isn't going to be number four to be lost if I can help it. The kids understand they're to stay clear of the jungle or there's an end to their play."

Because of the chance of losing the ball, the

boys decided not to use the bat. They left it near the ladder and spread out for a good game of catch. All efforts to lure Doc and Sandy down to join them failed. Doc said that if he could not collect he was darned if he would climb down the ladder just to throw a ball around. And Sandy insisted on remaining at the top of the ladder where he could watch the surrounding country for any signs of disturbance. But everything remained peaceful. The sun was warm. There was a light breeze. And soon the only sound was the smack of the ball as it hit leather.

Whiz—pop! Whiz—pop! The ball flew back and forth and Doc's and Sandy's heads moved from side to side, following its movement.

"Mighty professional boys we got there." Sandy finally broke the silence. "If we were all as good as that and if we had another team—we could have an Interplanetary Series right here."

"A lot of 'ifs' connected with that. If Elmer Clark hadn't been so crazy about being a space man, he could have played in big league baseball. Did you know that?"

"I've heard rumors," Sandy admitted. "But kinda like to forget 'em when I got a dirty job to be done. No hero worship for me. How about it, Elmer!" he yelled down at the boys. "What would you be doing if you weren't here?"

"He was gonna be a pitcher, weren't you, Elmer?" Jim Berry paused with the ball in his hand and wiped his forehead on his sleeve. "Say, let's show these guys your stuff. We'll set up a home planet and you pretend you're pitching a game."

"I dunno," Elmer said. "You're liable to drop it and it might go in the jungle."

"No, I won't! But we can put the bag right in front of the ship. If it gets by me, it'll bounce off the hull. Can't go in the jungle that way." Jim took off his jacket and folded it up to make a base. He put it down a few yards from the ship and stood behind it. "There you are. Now just imagine you got Bo Pearson or Kit Martin up there. He hit four home runs in the last series. How many would he get off you?"

Elmer obviously was itching to try. "Well, if it's O.K. with Sandy." He looked up to see what the machinist thought of using the ship for a backstop.

"Go ahead, boy," Sandy nodded.

"O.K. then. Get ready, Jim. And watch you don't get hit."

Elmer went into his wind-up and the ball whizzed over Jim's folded coat and zipped into Jim's glove.

"Boy, that was a hot one!" Jim was enthusiastic. "That must have been your fast one. Now let's see your drop ball and that slow curve you were telling me about."

Elmer obliged. As he got back into the feel of it, the balls came faster and with more accuracy. They curved, they dropped, they went fast and slow. Doc and Sandy watched with appreciation.

"How's your batting average? I bet you're hot there, too." There was no secret about how Jim felt about his pal. "Why don't we get old Doc and Sandy down here. With three of us, we could have batting practice."

"Heck, no! That way we'd lose the ball sure. Give it a little clout and it'd sail right over the trees."

"Turn the field around," pleaded Jim. "Put Sandy out there and he could stop anything before it got to the trees. And with Doc catching, I could pitch 'em to you all right. Just wind up like this . . ."

Jim was so fascinated with the picture of himself pitching that he failed to notice that Elmer was tying his shoelace. He went into the wind-up as he had seen Elmer do, and by the time he was aware that his friend was not ready for the catch, it was too late to do anything about it. The ball sailed over Elmer's head. Elmer let out a yell and leaped for it, too late. He turned just in time to see it disappear into the jungle.

A groan went up from both boys. Sandy was on his feet.

"Now that was real smart," he said. "But that's the end of it. There's to be no going into the jungle after it. That's understood and agreed upon and unless . . ."

He stopped in mid-sentence, his mouth open for the unspoken word. At that moment the ball came sailing back out of the jungle, propelled by some unseen force directly toward Elmer, who automatically reached up and caught it.

It hit his glove with a loud smack, and then there was utter silence. Doc was standing up, too. All four men were staring unbelievingly at the jungle. Then they all spoke at once.

"Where'd that come from? Who threw it? Did you see that?"

With sudden determination, Elmer threw the ball back to the approximate spot in the trees from which it had come. In no time it reappeared, this time coming to Jim. He did not have to move to catch it.

"I don't believe any of this," he said.

Sandy was roaring at the boys to get up the ladder quick before anything unexpected could happen. But there was a light of determination in Elmer Clark's eyes.

"Give me that ball," he said.

Jim tossed it over, and Elmer, standing halfway between the ship and the jungle, began systematically to thrown the ball into the trees. Each time it came back to him, he threw it a little nearer the edge until finally a drop ball went careening toward the trees and fell short a foot in front of them. There was a wild thrashing in the underbrush and a creature shot out of the jungle, caught the ball just before it hit the ground, and collapsed in a heap in the grass.

Doc, who was peering through his binoculars, let out a shout.

"A reptile! A green dinosaur! Just as that first crew reported. But I never expected to see one catch a baseball!"

"It was a darned good catch," Jim said. "If I'd tried it, I'd have tripped in all those vines."

"Elmer Clark!" yelled Sandy. "Come back away from that thing! You're disobeying orders and it's going down in the record!"

But Elmer stood where he was. His face lit up in a wide grin and he held out his hand.

"Throw it here, Hotstuff," he said.

"Hotstuff" picked himself up off the ground. As he stood up, it became apparent that he was as tall as Elmer. He stood easily on his hind legs with some assistance from a small tail. He was entirely covered with tiny green scales, and at first glance it seemed that one of the smaller dinosaurs had been resurrected on this distant world. But here the similarity ceased. The front legs of Earth's dinosaurs were so small as to be almost useless and their heads were extremely small in comparison with their bodies. This creature had well developed arms, ending in five-fingered hands, and the head was in proportion. In fact, it was not a reptile head at all, but resembled more one of our primates, with eyes set well in front for stereoscopic vision.

Doc Bender let out a long whistle. "Fascinating, Sandy, fascinating! Makes you wonder what happened to evolution on this planet. Must have skipped the mammals entirely—or perhaps this *is* a mammal that kept certain reptilian features, like the scales. Though how they could do that and regulate their body temperature . . . Probably the scales are quite different from those of our reptiles."

"Keep your theories for later," growled Sandy. "They're obviously some of the critters that smashed up our other expeditions, and whether they play baseball or not, they're dangerous. We've got to get those boys back into the ship!"

"You're a better man than I am if you can."
Doc sat down at the top of the ladder and trained
his glasses on Elmer's new friend. "Doesn't look
especially dangerous to me. But you've got to
remember, this may be the young of the species.
If they're like our dinosaurs, the adults should be
formidable."

The reptile threw the ball to Elmer. He approached, his hands held out, evidently eager to
play. His original shyness seemed to vanish as
Elmer threw it back—now high, now low, now
fast or slow or to the side. He caught it every time.

"Jumping jets! He's a natural!" cried Elmer.
"Look at that! He can't miss. Say, Jim. Let's
see what he thinks of a bat."

Jim ran for the bat, despite continuing bellows
from Sandy. Elmer took it and began batting the
ball lightly in the visitor's direction. That clinched
the matter. With a delighted gurgle, the creature
rushed upon Elmer, holding out its arms for the
new toy. Elmer demonstrated. He let him hold it
and swing it. He showed him how to bat the ball
to Jim. The animal was beside itself with joy. It
jumped up and down. It turned a somersault.
And all of a sudden it stopped and let out a low,
hissing whistle. There was more crashing in the
underbrush and before Elmer and Jim knew what
was happening they were surrounded by seven

miniature dinosaurs, all demanding a chance at the ball and bat.

Sandy took one horrified look, fell over Doc Bender, and rushed through the air lock to the communications room.

"Gene!" he yelled. "Lieutenant! Come quick! We're being attacked by natives! The boys are surrounded!"

Fairless emerged from his cubbyhole.

"What's going on?" he demanded. "Do you have to make all that noise? They're just beginning to get somewhere. Located a nice deposit, Harlow thinks. I don't want to lose contact."

"But the boys!" Sandy choked. "The dinosaurs! They wouldn't obey orders, and now there's at least seven of them . . ."

"Seven what?"

"Seven dinosaurs. They were jumping on Elmer and Jim."

"What! Wait a minute . . ." Gene turned back to his earphones. "Hello . . . hello! Oh, never mind. Here, take over, will you. No—get the guns. Get the blaster. Hurry!"

Gene was already on his way to the hatch. When he pushed out and stood beside Doc, he was prepared for the worst. But fantastic as was the sight that met his eyes, there seemed to be nothing wrong with either Jim or Elmer. Instead,

they were surrounded at a respectful distance by seven of the strangest creatures Gene had ever seen and Elmer was saying:

"Now this is home planet. Home."

His listeners all said "Om" after him, with varying degrees of inflection.

"This is first." Elmer ran to a stone a short distance away, and held up one finger. "This is second." He put down his jacket (Jim's jacket was still serving as home) and held up two fingers. "This is third." He put down his cap and held up three fingers. "And then you get back to home planet and you have a run. Now you take the bat like this, and the podres pitches it, you hit it, you run to first, and the podres throws the ball to first, and if they touch you, you're out."

This was all illustrated by hitting the ball to Jim, running to first, and getting there just as Jim threw the ball to him.

"Understand?"

There was a roar as all the pupils started to jabber at once. Their voices were somewhat between a squeak and a bark, but altogether they added up to a lot of noise. But a louder roar boomed from the top of the ladder.

"What in space do you think you're doing?" Gene Fairless held onto the railing and wondered if he were losing his mind.

Elmer and Jim came to attention at the tone of their officer's voice.

"Teaching them to play baseball, sir. They seem to like it a lot."

"It's going to be an interesting experiment, Gene," said Doc Bender. "If they can learn baseball without knowing the language, it will give us a key to their I.Q."

"Very interesting, I'm sure. Especially if we ever get back home with the facts."

Just then Sandy squeezed through the air lock. There was no room for him on the ladder outside, but he stuck out his head and one arm.

"Here are the guns, sir," he said. "Can you and Doc handle them from there?"

Gene gave a disgusted snort. "Take 'em away!" he yelled. "No, wait. Give 'em to Doc. Both of you sit here and watch those idiots. If Doc tells you to shoot, shoot. But not before. It's your experiment, Doc. Now let me get through to communications right away. Space knows what they'll think if they're calling and I don't answer."

As Gene made his way back to the communications room, his mind was in confusion. Questions and answers chased each other with alarming rapidity. Was this the inimical life form that had destroyed the crews of the earlier starships and made Aldebaran 4 a proscribed world until such time as it could be invaded by force? They seemed to fit the scanty descriptions, but these specimens certainly did not look terrifying, avidly learning to play baseball from the ship's apprentices! Perhaps they were a gentler, friendlier species and the real threat was yet to come. In that case, it might be well to cultivate their friendship. Elmer was on the right track there. But was the boy being unnecessarily exposed to danger? Max had been so vehement in his instructions to stay in the ship and not contact the natives. Probably he, Gene, would be blamed for letting this situation develop.

Gene sat down at his instrument, determined to get instructions from his chief. Max would know what to do. To his surprise there was no answer to his call. He twiddled the dials.

"Starship calling! Starship calling! Come in X-3! Hey, Flum! Where are you? Come in, will you!"

Still no reply. Just the swishing kind of static they had here. Gene checked his power source. He checked all possible breaks in his instrument. Everything was functioning as usual—except that he could not contact Richie Flum. What was Richie doing? He remembered the way the man had staggered into the jungle, tripping over the rocks, only just catching his balance on a log. Perhaps the big goof fell down and smashed the talk-box. He sometimes wondered how anyone like Richie got onto an expedition like this. But he was a good communications man. Even as Gene considered the possibility of a sprained ankle for Richie, he knew that the man would protect the talk-box with his life.

Gene was about to go out and get Sandy to help recheck the instrument, when he heard a faint voice in his earphones. He clapped them back on and turned up the volume.

"Gene! Gene! Answer me!"

"Starship here! What's happened, Richie? Where you been?"

"What the heck happened to you? I've been trying and trying . . . Interrupted for a few minutes . . . No time now. Get this, Gene . . ."

"Get me Max," Gene broke in. "Put him on, will you? I got important news for him."

"I can't put him on, Gene. That's what I'm telling you. They got him! They got all the others! They're coming after me now!"

"Who got him?" cried Gene, although he knew the answer before he heard it.

"The natives. Now don't get excited, Gene. Take it easy and do what I tell you. Here are Max's orders."

"You take it easy," Gene said. "And tell me what these natives look like."

"They're just like Doc Bender described 'em. They ambushed us. And they mean business. Max says you're to raise ship at once. Get out of here and back to Rigel 3. That's orders, Gene. That's Max's orders. That's all I've time . . . They're coming! They're com . . . Oh, no!"

The last word ended in a scream and then there was the crashing of static noises as though the talk-box were being rudely smashed.

Gene sat at the instrument for a few more minutes. He turned the dials and called over the transmitter: "Starship calling! Come in, Richie! Come in!"

But there was no answer and he knew in his heart there would be none.

"Take it easy," he muttered. "Don't get excited! My eye!"

He hurried to the air lock. Doc and Sandy moved down the ladder to make room for him at the top. Out in the clearing the "natives" had spread out in an approximation of a baseball outfield, and Elmer was standing in the center, demonstrating the pitching technique to one of the lizard-like men.

"You see, if you throw from up here and back here, you get much more speed into it. And if you hold it like this, there's any number of ways you can twist it."

"How do you expect him to understand that?" Jim was standing in the catcher's place. "Give him a demonstration he can see."

"All in good time," said Elmer. "Take it easy."

Gene winced as he heard the repetition of that phrase.

"Doc, if these are the young of the species, their parents are a lot meaner. Our search party has been captured."

Doc took a firmer hold on the ladder rail. He had the feeling that he was about to plunge to the bottom. He heard Sandy say, "Not all of 'em! It's not possible!" And he listened in a numb sort of way while Gene described his conversation with Richie.

"And what are we supposed to do now?" Sandy asked when Gene had finished.

"We're to raise ship right away and go back to Rigel 3."

"We *will* not!"

"It's what we agreed to do before the search party left."

"When this was only a hypothetical case," murmured Doc.

"But," said Sandy, "but . . . we can't do that to those guys!"

"Doc," Gene said, "we've got to think . . . I wonder if we don't have something here that alters the case."

He looked out at the clearing just as "Hotstuff" went into a very creditable imitation of a wind-up and sent the ball flying across "home planet" to Jim's waiting glove.

"Did you see that!" yelled Elmer.

"You couldn't have done better yourself," cried Jim. "He's going to make a podres all right!"

"Never saw anyone learn so fast in my life."

Doc was staring down at the two apprentices. "What do you call him a podres for?" he asked. "I thought he was the pitcher."

Jim stopped under the ladder to call up his answer. "There was a guy named Podres," he yelled, "way back at the beginning of the game. I don't know just what he did, but now all the top pitchers are called podres." He stepped back to catch the ball as the lizard-like man sent it winging over the plate.

"I see," said Doc Bender.

"I wish I could see what we're going to do," said Gene.

"Hey—I got an idea!" Sandy sounded almost cheerful again. "If these are the children of the natives that got hold of Max, why don't we do a bit of kidnaping. You know, hostages . . . ransom

. . . that way we get our men back. Then we turn these guys loose and scram."

"That would be the worst thing we could do," Doc said. "Any shooting, any aggression, would just finish us off. No, we've got two emissaries of good will in the boys down there. If we do anything at all, they're our trump cards."

"Suppose these are no relation to the big ones?" asked Sandy. "Suppose they're just a minor form of life, as you might say?"

"That's something we ought to try to find out," Gene replied. "Do you suppose those kids could get the idea over to their playmates?"

"They seem to have done all right explaining the rules of baseball." Doc leaned over the railing and raised his voice to holler. "Say, boys, can you bring him over here for a minute? Your patty . . . or potty . . . we want to ask a question."

Jim stopped the game with a look of disgust. "I keep telling you he's a podres," he said as he mounted the ladder. "What is it this time?"

But when they heard Gene's story of what had happened to the exploring party, the boys forgot about their game.

"I can't believe it!" Elmer said. "They seem so friendly."

"Just imagine them twice as big," Doc pointed out.

"The question is, are these relatives or something entirely different?" Gene asked.

"Can they be got to fight on our side?" Sandy asked. "You kids have to find out."

"That's a little more complicated than baseball." Elmer looked thoughtful. "I have it! Paper and pencil. Jim's a pretty good artist." When these were brought out, he shoved them at his friend. "Get busy," he ordered. "Draw a picture of 'Hotstuff.' And now one of me. It doesn't have to look like me . . . just a guy holding a ball. Fine. Now on this sheet draw 'Hotstuff' twice as big. And maybe a man stretched out at his feet."

"Don't let's get too gory," Doc said. "We don't know if anyone's hurt yet."

"If you heard Richie on the talk-box . . ." Gene began.

"Oh, Richie!" Elmer exclaimed. "Gimme those!" He grabbed the drawings and scrambled down the ladder to the waiting lizards.

First he showed "Hotstuff" the drawing of himself, and it so enthralled the young animal that every other consideration was forgotten. The picture was handed around among all seven reptiles and commented upon with the barks and hissings that made up their language.

When the excitement had worn off, Elmer showed them the drawing of the boy with the ball and bat. This started another series of barks and squeaks, and when the third drawing of the hypothetical adult was produced, the din became terrific. Elmer wondered if he couldn't have used a less exciting way of putting his ideas across. They became so vociferous that despite his feeling of good fellowship for the strange creatures, he retreated to the foot of the ladder. Otherwise, he might not have heard Jim's yell from above and the sudden crashing from the jungle.

Elmer climbed hastily to what he considered a safe height and then turned to look. He saw the trees moving far back in the forest, the movement coming nearer like a ripple from a stone cast into a pool.

The creatures below were suddenly quiet. Then the trees parted and a figure of enormous stature moved out into the clearing. The watchers gasped as it advanced towards the ship. There were certain important differences, but the men could not escape the feeling that they were face to face with Tyrannosaurus Rex.

Elmer scrambled the rest of the way up the ladder to join Jim at the top. He was aware of the white faces of the men framed in the narrow opening of the air lock. Then from below he heard his name called in an unbelievable, guttural roar.

The question of the relationship of the big and

little lizards was answered almost at once. The giant animal was pushing "Hotstuff" toward the ship just as a parent might push a reluctant child. Without doubt it was aware of the consternation its appearance created and was trying to use the little fellow to bridge the gap.

"El-mer!" Hotstuff echoed. "El-mer! Let-ter!"

"That drawing wasn't such a bright idea after all," Elmer said. "What's he waving it at me for?"

"It's not the drawing he's waving," said Doc. "It's something else. Looks like a letter all right."

Elmer peered down the ladder. There did seem to be writing on the paper.

"What'll I do, Lieutenant? Shall I get it?"

"By all means, if you can do so without *it* getting you! Bring it inside where we can all look at it."

Very gingerly, and keeping an eye on the huge reptile, Elmer inched down the ladder and accepted the folded sheet of paper from "Hotstuff." Then he quickly climbed back into the ship.

"It's addressed to you, Lieutenant. And unless these creatures write English, it must be from one of our party."

Gene took it unbelievingly and without hesitation read it aloud.

"It's from Max all right. He says, 'Dear Gene:

This smells like a trap to me, so use your judgment. This character knows a little English. From a member of the first expedition, since dead. He insists that we have been playing a wonderful new game. What in space have you been doing back there? He says that they're all crazy about games and if we'll teach them this one, they'll let us all go and everything will be cozy. If there's anything in this, better take them up on it. But if it looks like a trick, don't fall for it. Blast off and forget us—which you should have done already if you'd obeyed orders. Max.' "

There was a short silence as Gene stared at his crew and they all looked back at him.

"Well, Doc," he said at last. "You're the public relations expert. What do you make of it? Is it a trick?"

"I think," Doc answered, "that an ounce of sportsmanship is worth a pound of guns. We ought to have a ballplayer on every ship that goes out to the stars."

TIGER BY THE TAIL

by Gene L. Henderson

Will Crowder had always thought that working jigsaw puzzles was fun; but not any more. For instance, he thought, scatter the pieces in a hundred acre field. Then, just to make it more interesting, have them change positions while you were looking for a key piece.

That was kid stuff, he thought to himself wryly as he studied the diagram spread all over the work table. To make it more difficult, eliminate the field and scatter the pieces in space in varying orbits around Earth. Assemble this do-it-yourself kit and you came up with a nice space station. The first one, incidentally.

Perhaps this change of pace would do him good. Anyway, he could blame it all on his slogan, "We can build anything, anywhere." He had proved it under trying circumstances in various parts of the world. There had been that one dam in a bit of contested territory between two small countries. It had been completed while he fought off the armies of both factions and then threatened to blow it up himself if the sum promised by his customer was not paid immediately.

The United States Department of Defense had contacted him. A general had said, "We like the aggressiveness of your company, Mr. Crowder. The job we have in mind is going to take that quality, plus imagination. Of course the odds are that you won't be able to do the job the first time, but it has to be tried and I believe that you have the best chance."

Will had never been able to determine if the general had used psychology on him or had hit upon the idea of a challenge accidentally. Either way, the very thought that someone thought he might not be able to do the job had made it irresistible.

A chill settled his enthusiasm when he heard that he was expected to assemble a space station, but pride in his ability alone would have been sufficient to keep him agreeable to accepting the job. He signed the contract and the Defense Department immediately kept its first part of their working agreement.

All of the parts were blasted into space using production line ICBM propulsion units. There were setbacks and failures of course but, for each failure, other missiles were waiting with the necessary parts.

On paper, it sounded like a simple job since the pure mechanics of assembly, even in space, were not especially difficult. All he had to do was to bring the pieces together so that they could begin work on them.

Training astronauts to new trades had sometimes been easier than taking skilled workmen and qualifying them for space, but that problem too had been met and conquered in a minimum of time. Getting the men into space was not easy, but it had been done with maximum assurance that they would return safely. There were even rescue rockets backing up rescue rockets. The United States was still advocating the value of human life over mere accomplishments.

He glanced out a port of the partially completed station, then closed his eyes quickly. It took a bit of mental reorientation. The station was tumbling but this was not important insofar as assembly was concerned. All he had to do was keep telling himself that the station was actually solid and unmoving, that earth and other parts of the station were tumbling around him.

He saw that he was almost in the communication zone and turned on the equipment to warm up. He would have forty minutes for tight beam instructions inside the zone.

He looked at the list of sections needed next and hoped that the computers down on Earth could give him coordinates and the time for the pick-ups before they lost contact. The sturdy little tow rockets could handle just about anything once they had found it.

Will opened his circuit and began calling,

"Hello, Home Base. Hello, Home Base. This is Way Station calling, this is Way . . ." A burst of static interrupted him and a heavy voice boomed out.

"Way Station, we receive you loud and clear. This is an emergency. I say again, this is an emergency." Will felt a sudden lump in his throat.

"Go ahead, Home Base," he called back in a clear, steady voice, much to his surprise.

"The British launched their manned moon rocket," Home Base told him. "There was an explosion but they were able to go into orbit. Something jammed their ejection unit and they don't have enough fuel for a power letdown."

"How about a rescue rocket?"

"They didn't anticipate any trouble and don't have one. If we sent up another one it would jeopardize our operations and leave your men and you out on a limb if anything went wrong." There was a pause and Will broke the silence.

"I guess that leaves it up to us, then," he said.

"There's another problem," Home Base said slowly. "That's why we're leaving the decision entirely up to you."

"Go ahead, shoot."

"They're about fifty miles further out than you. That means a fuel problem as well as navigation since your ships weren't equipped for space journeys. If the rescue attempt is going to do any good, it has to be done before we can possibly shoot up more fuel in the supply rockets. It looks as if . . ."

"Wait," Will broke in. "You people down there can use your computers but how about the fuel the three tow rockets up here have, plus the little spare on hand? Give me the course coordinates." He looked at his watch. Only twenty minutes left before he would be out of range of Home Base.

"Better hurry it up," he warned, "not much time left."

"We already have the figures," Home Base said to his surprise.

"Then why waste all of this time?" he demanded, half irritated.

"The General said no pressure was to be put

on you," the operator half apologized. "It's your decision."

"Count me in," Will said promptly. "And, if you've gone this far already, you probably have their orbit computed and the coordinates I'll need for it."

"We have all the information you need. Is your tape recorder on?" Will nodded, then remembered this was no telecast. He was sending sound only and they could not see the nod.

"Sure," he said, "better hurry it up, though."

"Don't worry about the time element any more," he was told. "The communications facilities all over Earth are on our frequency. Everyone is cooperating for the rescue."

Home Base began sending the necessary instructions slowly and Will only half listened. He would have to play the figures back anyway and right now he had to call the two tow rockets back from their job of jockeying equipment back to the uncompleted station. His tow rocket, kept at the station for emergencies, could get the British rocket down to the Station where the other two could ease it up into the uncompleted hangar itself. This, as well as the control station, had been made pressure tight. It was only the living and recreation areas and the propulsion units that were still uncompleted.

Will had decided upon a plan that would bring the rescue try to all the people on Earth. He had wired the communications circuits so all that was said to the tow rockets was also transmitted down to Earth. People everywhere would be hanging onto every word.

Will briefed the four men manning the other two tow rockets and then set out on a trajectory that would put him in orbit with the disabled rocket with a minimum expenditure of the valuable fuel. Various tracking stations on Earth were able to vector him until he was within twenty miles of the orbit of the British rocket. Then a steady roar of interference broke all communications.

To turn back now would use so much fuel that another rescue attempt would be impossible even if there were time for it to be effective. Will decided to push on, using the last available data and interpolating as much as possible. He felt the same uneasiness he had as a child when he played a game of closing his eyes and trying to walk through a cluttered room without bumping into anything.

With a suddenness that startled him, his search radar began indicating objects again. There was still no signal from Earth and his radar could pick up nothing in that direction. Evidently he had passed through a band of interference and would now be able to find the target himself.

He tensed. On his screen was a blip. He carefully corrected his travel and was soon within visual sight of the target. It was a rocket all right and he began trying to raise it with his communicator. There was no answer but he thought that their frequencies were probably different. Still, he felt uneasy. Someone should have seen him and signalled in some manner. They could have . . . unless something had happened to them.

Speed was now essential. There was nothing he could do alone in space. He would have to tow the rocket to the Way Station as quickly as possible and then all the facilities of the station would be available for whatever assistance was required.

Fastening onto the rocket was no more complicated than hooking onto the pieces of the station he had been towing for weeks. He brought the rocket back through the belt of interference. He cut it loose, though, when within sight of the two other tow rockets and hurried back to Way Station to prepare for it.

"Calling Guide and Hunter. This is Station. Over," he broadcast from the control room when he had reached it.

"Got you, Station," came the reply from the tow rockets.

"Hook onto the rocket and bring it into the hangar."

"Roger, wilco."

Will became aware that there was nothing but a roar of static on the receiver set on the Earth frequencies. He remembered the band he had previously passed through and wondered if it were shifting? This was something for the science boys to research later. Once this rescue was over, he thought impatiently, he could get back to his job of construction.

Will watched carefully on his radar as the tow rockets and their prize slowly overtook him. The Way Station itself could not be jockeyed at the present except in extreme emergency to avoid collision. Later on when everything was in place, it would be strong enough to take the stress set up by alternately firing guide rockets. But now the tow rockets would have to nudge it close enough for his cables to take hold.

He thanked the foresight that had led them to mount all the accessories possible right at the beginning of construction. This had been done to keep them from drifting or cluttering up the space immediately around the Way Station. Now they could beam complete television coverage back to Earth. There was ample power with the solar generators in operation.

The next three hours were crammed with frantic and sometimes frustrating activity as the rocket was eased into position to be drawn up into the Way Station. Then it was inside, nestling in the adjustable cradle that more foresight had provided so that future and different sized space vehicles could be accommodated.

Will now had time to admire the beauty of the rocket's clean and functional lines. It looked better than he had thought it would. His eyes narrowed. Strange, he could see no signs of an explosion aft on the rocket. Perhaps all the damage was internal.

While he waited for the crews of the tow rockets to emerge, he tried tuning the receivers again. The static was beginning to lessen. That would make it possible for their telecast to reach Earth also. He had the cameras all focussed on the rocket, covering the main angles so that they would not have to be manned.

The four men in the two tow crews came in through the air lock into the hangar and began removing their suits, grinning self-consciously into the cameras. Will peered through the glass separating the control room from the hangar. He motioned towards the rocket and they nodded affirmatively. One had gone to the side of the rocket and began pounding on it to indicate to those inside, if they were capable of hearing, that they could now emerge.

Fragments of voices began coming through in the receivers and Will called Home Base.

"Calling Home Base; this is Station," he called, a note of triumph in his voice. "We have the rocket cradled in the hangar and will either get the crew to emerge or force our way in to aid them."

"What happened up there, what happened up there?" someone at Base shouted excitedly. "What have you done?"

"What do you mean?" Will asked, taking a startled glance at the rocket to assure himself that it was still there.

"The British have just notified us that their rocket crew was able to eject safely and that the rocket itself crashed in Canada. They say they have no knowledge of the ship you pulled in. And it's definitely not anything from previous shots, they're all accounted for."

"Impossible," Will exploded. "It's right here, everyone can see it. Why we can even . . ."

"Way Station, you don't understand. There are no spare parts up there. We know where all of our stuff is."

"Then if it's not theirs and not ours, whose is it?" Will asked. He cast another anxious eye on their prize, other strange details in its construction now clamoring for attention.

"Or what is it?" his speaker bounced back. "You'll soon find out."

Will watched open-mouthed along with the rest of the world as a long narrow hatch began to slide back.

It was definitely too narrow for a human body.

THE SMALLEST MOON

by Don Wilcox

Doc signaled us to assemble in the spaceship. This was it, the call to blast off back to the solar system. Our Explorer 889, many times faster than light, was all set for the return flight.

We scrambled up the ladder. Our air locks stood wide open. This final planet of our sky survey had been one of the most pleasant, its air and gravity almost "normal," its three moons magically beautiful. We paused for a last look at the night scene. We had taken a fancy to the smallest moon, misty with atmosphere, and wished we could have gone to it. Anyway we had photographed it thoroughly, gathering data for a new sky atlas. Now—time to be off.

"Come on, chimp!" We whistled to our mascot, the one member of our party still outside.

Inside, Doc stood calm and massive in gray while we took our places at the circular table.

Percussion, the chimpanzee, strolled in. We were all aboard, four men and a chimp.

Doc gave Percussion a signal. The smart chimp touched the proper buttons; the retractable ladder and platform folded into the ship and the air locks closed. The chimp swung modestly to his shelf. "Thank you, Percussion." Then Doc turned to address us. "Be seated. . . . Well!"

This was routine, a quick "blast" from Doc before we blasted off. We sat in silence while Doc paced.

"Gentlemen, you act as though you haven't had your fill. I know what you're thinking. I know what you want: a short stop on that smallest moon before we blast for home. Right?"

I glanced at Dillo, our young geologist, who lifted an eyebrow as if to ask: Is the boss really going to give us a break—an unscheduled stop? I shook my head. No use getting our hopes up. An excursion under Doc was all work and no play, and how we had worked! No one had ever heard of Doc giving his crew an hour's caper on a strange moon just for a bonus. He had the sternness of a veteran spaceman, though he was only thirty-two, and he possessed one marked peculiarity: He never walked out on the surface of a planet or satellite if he could avoid it. You rarely saw him in a spacesuit. In fact, we often wondered if he were afraid. Afraid of light gravity, maybe.

Doc scowled at us. "I warn you, an extra stop would take time. I expect to get you home on schedule. We'll be busy with book work all the way. You, Dillo, you've no time for skylarking."

"Yes, sir."

"I'm not criticizing. You've handled the geology well. But you're still stalled on planets thirteen, fourteen, and fifteen—those *alondolite* masses."

"My hypotheses are all wrong," Dillo said frankly. "I've worked till I'm black in the face."

"You'll need every minute of time."

"I need a breather," Dillo said.

Doc turned to me. "You, Merlin, you're up to your ears in unfinished reports. And you, Gary—"

We sensed Gary's tension. We all knew his trouble—mathematics. He was the youngest of our party, only sixteen. As a pilot, he was learning fast. But he was hopelessly behind in his lessons. Doc had accused him of inventing excuses to escape studying. He was a large, awkward boy, as strong as a powerhouse, too restless to concentrate on his books.

Doc glanced at his watch and suddenly chopped

off. "Enough of talk. We'll put it to a vote. It takes three out of four to carry. You first, Merlin. Shall we make a quick stop on that certain moon—yes or no?"

"Yes," I said.

"Dillo?"

"Yes."

"Gary?"

"No."

We all stared at Gary. He gave an embarrassed smile. "Two hundred and thirty-five math problems to go."

Dillo groaned. Doc said, "Well!" and for an instant the breath had gone out of him. I said, "Doc, you haven't voted yet."

Then Doc knocked the wind out of the rest of us. "I vote yes. Bonus for good behavior. Carried! Be ready for blast-off in three minutes."

Three minutes later we were cushioned and ready. As always, Percussion, although harnessed, beat his fists right up to zero like a symphony on the kettle drums. A shudder. A roar. We leaped!

We recovered immediately. The moon was so close, it was only a "snail-pace" hop of less than two hours. "Just time for a home-cooked meal," Dillo said, and clacked "down" to the kitchen on his gravs. This was an event to celebrate, not with food pills but home cooking. When the chimp scampered back from the kitchen, put-puttering his lips, we knew it was going to be pancakes. Dillo had been joking over our silly slogan again, "When pink pills pall, pass the purple pancakes." Leave it to Percussion to try to imitate. Good little fellow! We always shuddered when we had to use him as a guinea pig, letting him run the risks on the new worlds before we took chances. Now he brought us plates of food.

Doc refused. He was lost in his papers—had put on his "ice-cap," to use Dillo's geological phrase. This meant we were strictly on our own as our ship coasted "down."

Gary perspired at the controls. This moon's gravitation was so slight. Then, "We're all right," he said. We came down smoothly.

Not until we actually completed the landing could we see the surface. Through the final miles of descent the fog of bluish-white atmosphere had been blinding. Now, through the visors, we could barely see a wilderness of thin colors through the whiteness. The lower end of our ship cushioned itself in the spongy vegetation; there was a slight quivering thump, and we had settled.

"Can't see more than seventy or eighty yards," Dillo said, studying the visor. "Quiet, Percussion. Don't get nervous yet."

The chimp seemed to know he would soon be

used for routine tests of air and gravity. He danced around with excitement. Dillo and I hurriedly adjusted our spacesuits.

"Get into 'em, Percussion," Dillo ordered. Smart chimp, he fairly leaped into his brightly colored outfit. He could dress himself, all but the latching-up. Since low atmospheric pressure might deal death to man or chimp, we double-checked his tamper-proof fastenings.

Gary sat at his desk, helmet, mittens, oxygen tank untouched. "Coming, Gary?" Dillo asked.

Gary shook his head. "Two hundred and thirty-five problems."

Doc looked up sharply. "Get along, fellow. Give Percussion some exercise." Gary grinned and reached for his helmet.

The chimp tugged at Doc's arm. He never seemed to learn there were times when Doc wouldn't budge. He held out a pancake as a bribe.

"He's coaxing you, Doc," I said. "Want to come?"

Doc ignored my question. He kept an eye on us as we pressured our suits. His voice came through our electronic diaphragms. "You have ninety minutes. Have fun and don't get lost."

We pressed the button for the retractable platform to unfold. One at a time we moved through the air locks, and there we were! The little moon was all ours.

We couldn't see far, the atmosphere was so thick and white. Percussion batted at his helmet as if he thought his eyes had gone steamy. What we could discern was a lumpy surface of sponge-like vegetation, green and pink and yellow. We gazed and laughed. It had the same harmless look it had had from a distance. And it *was* harmless, except for the *lack of gravity*.

We weren't standing on the platform, we were clinging to it; and Gary was holding tight to Percussion. The chimp had picked up something in his gloved hand on the way out—a piece of pancake. We laughed to see him make a sour face because he couldn't eat it—on account of his helmet, of course. He gave it a toss.

It went up, and up, and up.

It cut a straight course through the thick atmosphere, bound for outer space.

Gary hugged Percussion closely. "That's just how you'd go, funny face, if we turned you loose. You know how much you weigh on this moon? Less than a toy balloon. So hold tight!"

Actually, according to Gary's figures, a two-hundred-pound man on this moon, which had a diameter of four hundred miles, would weigh not quite half an ounce. No wonder we all got busy and snapped the safety hitches onto our belts.

The hitches were simply long leashes, similar to a leash for a pet dog. Attached to the platform were four of these hitches, allowing each of us a roving radius of a hundred and fifty feet. That was enough distance in this thick air to walk out of sight of each other, as we soon discovered. These lines, not chain but light, tough rope, too strong to be broken, were all one needed to be sure he would not float off in space when he stepped or jumped. You would bounce upward, naturally, because you weighed almost nothing, and there was enough power in the push of your little toe to thrust you high into the air. Fortunately, you would rise only a hundred and fifty feet, at which point the hitch, extended to its limit, would allow you to go no farther, and you would bounce back to the surface like a rubber ball.

The mechanism was simple. When not in use, a hitch would wind itself onto its own spool, at the touch of a button. All four spools were built into the frame of the retractable platform.

Since there were four hitches, and Doc apparently meant to stay inside, we attached the fourth to the chimpanzee. Thus we were all equipped to venture forth independently, like a quartet of animated, air-filled balloons on strings.

"There you go, 'Cussie. You're safe. We'll call you back for the real business later. Run along."

Zip! Percussion was off like a circus clown on springs. Zip, zip—we were right after him. For minutes it was like a slapstick comedy. We'd jump; we'd swing out to the ends of our lines as if we were flying. We'd bump harmlessly. We'd tangle. We'd throw shreds of sponge-plant at each other, and the pieces would sail off into the whiteness overhead, never to return. Without the hitches, we'd have done the same. We felt about as substantial as soap bubbles.

Percussion made a game of leaping over us, cutting a shallow arc as if he were beginning to get the feel of that faint gravitational pull. He was enjoying himself hugely.

As long as we were close together, the sound waves from our electronic diaphragms were carried by the air. This saved us from having to turn on our intercoms; which meant that Doc, inside the ship and busy with his own thoughts, wasn't bothered by our shouting.

Now we came together for a purpose. The chimp was to be our guinea pig. Where was he? Lost in the fog! He was playing his own game of hide-and-seek, enjoying the protective coloration of his space suit. Dillo touched one of the buttons at the platform, and the spool for the fourth hitch reeled in the line slowly. The chimp, attached to it, was dragged in, and you knew from the look of his beady eyes that he thought he was going to be punished for hiding.

"Everything's fine, 'Cussie. We want to give you a breath of moon air, that's all," Dillo said. "Just a sample. If you drop dead, we'll never forgive ourselves."

Actually, we believed we were taking no risks, from what Dillo had already ascertained about the atmosphere.

We were careful. Gary unlocked the tiny motor attached to the chimp's oxygen tank, and let it buzz for a few seconds. Moon air was thus pumped into the chimp's oxygen supply, to be inhaled within his helmet. "There. How's that? Any change?"

Percussie continued to breathe happily. We couldn't notice any effects.

"A little more," Dillo suggested. Gary added some more. "The rascal likes it."

For a few minutes we all watched the chimp closely. He drew deep breaths; he squinted good-humoredly and made a comical motion of trying to remove his space helmet for a full gulp of the outdoors. The lack of atmospheric pressure on this little moon could have killed him. But he was safe. The helmet was fastened on securely, chimp-proof.

Then we tried the air ourselves, pumping it into our back-borne oxygen tanks. Dillo took only a little at first. Then he stepped it up. Gary and I did the same. We breathed deeply.

"Like home cooking," Dillo said.

It gave you a strange sensation, like tropical fruits and flowers. My mind suddenly filled with poetic words. There was a certain poem about the deep jungle—

"Listen, fellows, I can recite some poetry."

Dillo's look withered me. Had I said something absurd? I took another breath. Ah, poetry! I really *should* recite—

I began. That mysterious old jungle poem was just the thing. Loudly, with expression—

"Cut it!" Dillo yelled at me. "Don't talk! I've got a brainstorm coming up."

"Me, too," Gary said. "*Quiet!*"

No appreciation. All right, I'd walk off—or rather, bounce off—and recite to myself. But they didn't know what they were missing. Man, oh man, how I did recite poetry! I lounged on the lumps of sponge-plant, like a lazy lizard in the sun, and ripped and roared through all the poems I'd ever forgotten.

The strange thing was, I remembered them perfectly. Just a few years before, I'd stumbled miserably over these jumbles of words in school. Now they came to me like crystal. Nothing like this ever happened to me before. I must be a new kind of genius—just waking up to it! I must go back and tell Dillo and Gary.

I skipped over the sponge clumps weightlessly. "Dillo!" I met him near the platform. "Dillo, I've got to tell you—where are you going?"

"Inside. Don't stop me." He leaped to the top of the ladder.

I was beside him. "Anything wrong?"

"Everything's right," he said excitedly. "Got to get this brainstorm down on paper before it gets away."

"Poetry?"

"Poetry, my eye! Planets. Those *alondolite* masses. You know—thirteen, fourteen, and fifteen. I've got a new hypothesis. It's a flash. This air— I'll tell you later." He unfastened himself from the hitch, which floated to the foot of the ladder as weightlessly as a strand of spider web. Signaling for the air locks to open, he said, "Keep an eye on Gary and Doc till I get back."

"Doc?" I was puzzled, remembering that Doc had stayed inside.

"Doc came out," Dillo added. "He went off

that way." Dillo gave an indefinite gesture and then was gone as the outer air lock closed.

I stared at the platform. Something disturbed me. Our four safety hitches. The first lay empty. Dillo just dropped it, and absently I touched the button to rewind it on its spool. The second was attached to my own belt. The third led out to Gary, sitting within view about thirty yards away. The fourth, which trailed out of sight, had been attached, when last seen, to the chimp.

Then where was Doc?

I'm not given to sudden alarms. My thoughts don't fire at rocket speed. I stood there; I counted the lines twice before the first pang of panic went through me. Foolishness. Doc must have taken Percussie's line. If so, Percussie was with him, naturally.

But just to be sure I snapped on my radio. "Doc . . . Calling Doc . . . Are you there on the fourth? . . . Calling Doc . . ."

No answer. I touched the wind-up button, the spool turned, and the fourth line came reeling in. The end appeared, gliding over the mounds, but no one was on it. I stared. Foolishness! Doc must have gone back inside and taken 'Cussie with him. Why worry? Still—

I bounced down toward Gary. "What's happened to the chimp? He's not on his line."

"Don't bother me."

"The chimp," I said. "He's gone!"

"Dillo must have him."

"Not Dillo. I just saw Dillo."

"Doc, then," Gary said and went on mumbling to himself.

I shook him. "Have you *seen* Doc?"

Gary's expression brightened. "I'd *like* to see him. I've got a surprise. Those problems! They're clicking. I've worked five in my head, just sitting here. It's this air—good, huh?" He touched the oxygen motor. Smiling like a schoolboy with an A on his grade card, he worked a problem for me. Then he talked of cube root. "It's easy. You take the number, 21,642,171. Write it down in your mind and—"

He broke off, for we both saw Dillo bounding toward us. Dillo was shouting.

"Who let the chimp off the line?"

"Didn't Doc take him inside?" I asked.

"Doc's not inside. I told you he came out."

"You didn't tell me where he went. Did he have a hitch?"

"He followed the fourth one out of sight. The last I saw he was running the line through his hand. Look, all three of us are hitched, one, two, and three. But there's the fourth, wound up on its spool. Where's Doc? Where's the chimp?"

We snapped on our radios and began calling. We got no answer. We all went pale, thinking the worst.

I tried to be optimistic. "If he's floating off in space, you *know* he's radioing, or trying to. He must be around somewhere."

Dillo muttered. "But *is* he? I've got a notion he's unsafe outside the ship, the way he sticks so tight to his desk . . . *Calling Doc . . . Calling Doc!*"

By this time Gary had taken a quick run back into the ship, to search every part, just to make sure. He came back with an extra piece of rope, tying a lasso into it, as if he had some notion of throwing it out into the void and snaring our two missing members.

Something clicked in my thoughts. "I know what the chimp's done. He's let himself loose."

"You know he can't do that," Dillo scoffed. "Those hitches are chimp-proof."

"Nothing's proof in this air," I said. "After the deep breath we gave him—if his brain lighted up the way mine did—"

"Mine, too," Gary said.

"Makes sense," Dillo admitted. "He's un-snapped himself. And he's either bounded off for the nearest star—or—*whew!*"

"Or what?"

"He might be just smart enough to do it twice!"

"What do you mean?"

Dillo's face was grave. "I mean—it could have happened! Just as he unfastened himself, he might have seen Doc coming along, with a hand on the line. Percussie might have hidden in the sponge and waited till Doc fastened the end onto his belt and thought himself safe to jump around. And then 'Cussie would have slipped up on Doc and unhitched him. That would be just the sort of playful trick 'Cussie would pull, and they'd both be floating off!"

We called again and then faced each other, three of the bluest spacemen you ever saw. Again I tried to be optimistic. "Doc's no amateur at this space game. He knew he'd be a featherweight in this gravity. He wouldn't let 'Cussie slip up on him."

Dillo's comment was utterly spiritless. "Why did I take a fancy to this moon?"

"It was my notion, too," I said.

"Mine, too," Gary said.

"You voted against it."

"I wanted to come. Doc knew it. That's why he voted the way he did. For me. *Hey! Percussie!*"

A brightly-colored object suddenly sailed past us in a shallow curve, like a drop-ball over home plate. Much bigger than a ball—and flappier! The chimp's gloved hands were flapping the air.

All three of us leaped after him. Dillo and I went high and bounded back foolishly. Gary followed in Percussie's course, called to him, and put the loop over him.

"Tie that leash on him, *good!*"

Gary knotted the short length of rope so that nothing less than a cutting blade would free it. Percussie, the imp, was as chummy as a long lost brother—until Dillo saw what he was up to.

"Hold on, Gary! *Don't move! You're loose!*"

That mischievous chimp! He'd learned the combination, all right. In a busy jiffy he'd undone the fastening of Gary's hitch. He was so happy over it, he beat his hands together and laughed like a clown. Now we knew he had cut Doc loose, too.

" 'Cussie! Where's Doc? Where's Doc?" we asked.

The mention of Doc made his eyes gleam, and that gleam was now our one ray of hope. We softened our tone.

"Take us to Doc, Percussie," Dillo said, now patting the little fellow. "We'll give you a pancake as soon as we find Doc. Pancake. Pass the purple pancake."

Gary manipulated the oxygen motor to feed

him more moon air. 'Cussie laughed and beat his knees and suddenly tried to leap away. Gary held the leash and the three of us followed, as if 'Cussie were a bloodhound.

The fog thinned a little. For the first time we could see a mist-filled depression beyond a ledge of vegetation. It was like an open stone quarry, cushioned with sponge. We stopped at the outer limits of our lines. We gazed, and the chimp was forgotten. There before our eyes—was *Doc!*

He was floating, fifteen feet below our level, only a pebble's toss away. He was wearing his neatly fitted space togs. There was no sign of any rope attached to him. There was hardly any sign of life, only the slight movement of his fingers, waving, finlike. He was swimming in the air, like a fish in a quiet pool.

Dillo gulped. "Do you fellows see it, too?"

Gary was mumbling mathematics, something about the foot-pounds required to circumnavigate a moon four hundred miles in diameter, if a man weighs forty-three hundredths of an ounce, and the resistance of air is—

"Turn off the math!" I bleated. "Get a hitch on him before he bounces off!" It was easier to give orders than to act. I couldn't take my eyes off the sight of Doc. It was Gary who offered to go back after the fourth hitch. He had tied Percussie to a sponge plant, so he was free—still he too was temporarily paralyzed by the strange situation. "He doesn't know he's loose! Don't frighten him!"

We were frozen by the thought. It was awful— to think that the chimp must have removed the hitch without Doc's knowing it—and there Doc was, enjoying himself as I had never seen him before. He hadn't discovered we were watching. He floated back and forth, barely touching one bank, bouncing back in an almost horizontal curve. More perfect muscular control I never hope to see. Yet one forceful kick would have sent him spinning off into the void.

Now he looked up and saw us. "Hello, fellows. Time to go?"

Dillo called in an unnatural voice, for his heart was right up in his voice box. "Hold on, Doc. Don't be scared, now. Get a grip on something, Doc. You're loose. The chimp did it. Hold on and we'll get a hitch."

Doc, looking at us curiously, gave a low laugh. Then, "Where *is* the chimp?"

"Picketed to a sponge plant." I pointed over my shoulder. *"Careful, Doc!"*

"Careful? Why? Can't I join you lads? This moon air gave me an urge to swim. Where you going, Gary? . . . *Don't* get a hitch for me. Just for Percussie—*Hey, Percussie! Stop it!*"

The chimp was *unlocking his space helmet!* He *couldn't*—but he was doing it! One more move and he'd commit chimp-slaughter. His blood vessels would pop like firecrackers.

All of us shouted. Doc leaped. Doc, with not a ghost of a safety line attached to him, darted past us like a human rocket. Darted true. He reached out and caught Percussie—snatched him into a bear hug—*and kept going!* The chimp's leash tore the sponge plant loose. It followed like an umbrella in the wind.

There was nothing in the world to stop them. Ahead was opaque atmosphere, and beyond that, the void. The ship loomed in the fog a little distance to the left. Doc was hugging the chimp and fighting to swim, but he couldn't hope to whip back to safety.

"Jump, everybody!" Dillo shouted. Gary had already jumped in straight pursuit—and jumping, he swung his arm and threw a wave into the slack of his line. The wave spiraled outward. Doc saw it coming, barely hooked it with his foot. His course glanced to the left, still on the rise. Would he pass within touch of the spaceship? His arm reached, his gloved fingers struck a glance off the surface of the skyward nose and thrust his course downward. He struck the surface, his body twisting for a calculated bounce, and the next thing we knew, he caught himself gracefully on the ship's platform.

By the time we got there, the chimp, snug in his arm, was grinning happily, playing a drum march on his securely fastened helmet.

We blasted off for the earth right on schedule.

We were speeding through space. Doc was at his desk, smiling to himself. Was he under his ice-cap? He turned and said casually, "Nice picnic." Percussion handed him a cold pancake. Doc ate it and gave the chimp a hug. Then, to Dillo and me, "What's all this talk about moon air? Poetry? Hypotheses?"

"That's how Percussie unhitched you," Dillo said. "He got his lungs full of this magic air."

"The chimp never unhitched me," Doc said. "Himself, maybe, but not me. I never use a hitch unless I weigh less than one-hundredth of an ounce. You get used to swimming in light gravity. You get hungry for it. Nice picnic. But about that air—don't you think you've overstated it? I'll admit it had a freshening effect. But what we all needed was a break. It was like an inspiration. So you jumped to the conclusion that the air—"

Doc broke off, staring across at Gary, who was working at his desk. "What's *he* doing, wearing that oxygen helmet inside the ship? Gary, what's the idea?"

Gary came over and placed a sheaf of papers under a clip on the circular table. "All done, sir. Two hundred and thirty-five problems. All checked." He grinned and pointed to the oxygen tank on his back. "Now I can take this stuff off."

SPACE LANE CADET

by William F. Hallstead III

Patrol trainee Stanley Hunter's gloved hands tightened on the control column as his Unit Commander's voice snapped in his earphones.

"Hunter! You're straggling—close in."

This was the order Stan had been dreading since take-off on the training mission into the stratosphere. Close in. Keep the formation tight.

He couldn't do it. He'd known he wouldn't be able to fly formation since he'd seen two of his fellow students smash their ships together not forty-eight hours ago. They had plunged through fifty miles of space into the North Atlantic, and B Flight had only five men left.

"Hunter," the ship-to-ship radio blurted. "Did you receive?"

Stan looked through the inch-thick plastic canopy. The six-rocket formation stretched away in echelon to the right. His was tail ship on the high end of the line of interceptors. The ships gleamed dully in the black sunlight of the upper stratosphere. They were sleek bullets of manganese-alloy, their smooth lines broken only by the stubby tips of the semi-retractable wings and tail assembly.

The six SF-7s, United States Strato Force, were built for patrol of U. S. Control Lane 4. The SF-7s were part of the patrol wing based at Niagara Falls. Each year, the Strato Force selected a small group of prospective patrol pilots. These trainees were sent to Niagara Falls where they were trained, tested, and finally assigned to the growing Space Lane Patrol.

At eighteen, tall, dark Stan Hunter was the youngest student thus far accepted at the training center. Stan had studied rocketry since he had learned to read. He soloed his first jet at sixteen and joined the Strato Force when he was old enough. Stan's progress through Niagara's training had been rapid. But two days ago, two of his fellow trainees had rammed each other in practice formation. The shock of this accident had done something to Stan. He could fly, but when it came to thinking about formation: no good.

Now the moment Stan feared had come. "Hunter! I'm giving you a direct order to close in. Acknowledge this order."

Stan tripped the mike button on the control stick. "Hunter. Wilco."

Desperately, he nudged the SF-7 to the right. The adjacent ship loomed larger as the space between them diminished to hundreds of feet. Stupid, Stan thought. Millions of miles of space around them, and the Strato Force stuck to its regulation requiring formation on all flights above the tropopause. Trainees lacked astrogational experience.

He was almost in close formation before the fear got him. His muscles jerked the controls. He veered two miles out before he could get a grip on himself and deflect to a straight course. Shaken and angry, Stan watched the five sister SF-7s cruise in smooth formation on his right, hanging against black outer space.

"What's the matter with you, Hunter?" Commander Wheaton's voice blasted. "Close in here. Now."

"I . . . I can't, sir," Stan blurted, and he felt shame in his cheeks.

"You're disobeying a direct order, Hunter. I'm going to recommend disciplinary action."

Stan tried to swallow the tightness in his throat.

This had happened so fast, he hadn't realized the consequences until now. Wheaton was strict—he'd washed out other trainees for less than Stan had done.

The curve of the earth's horizon flattened as the six rockets hurtled into the lower atmosphere and slowed their drive. At thirty-five thousand, six sets of retracted wings slid from their fuselage grooves and locked in place. The rockets took on the appearance of ordinary 1980 jet planes.

The crackle of atmospheric static filled Stan's earphones. Stretching his legs after this eight hour flight would be fine, but it meant an ordeal. He shuddered at the bitterness in Commander Wheaton's voice, but he still couldn't forget the two shattered patrol rockets. They haunted him.

The stratosphere ships plunged toward North America in a long diving arc. Ten thousand feet off the coast of New Jersey, the flight levelled out and the pilots shut off their cockpit pressurization and oxygen systems. They decelerated to Mach 2, twice the speed of sound. In minutes, the familiar white horseshoe of Niagara Falls drifted below the purple haze layer.

Stan banked into the two-mile final approach. The other planes of B flight were lining up on the broad ramp as he came in nose-high under partial power.

He flipped a lever, and the ship slowed as big flaps slid into the slipstream. The tricycle landing gear squealed on cement, and the pilot punched a snake-eye switch with two fingers. He lurched against his shoulder harness as the landing chute bellied from its tail compartment and cracked open. The plane slowed under the parachute's braking action.

Stan released the chute at the marked point on the runway where it would be picked up by a waiting truck. He ruddered the plane toward the flight line.

As he slid back the heavy canopy and climbed from the cockpit, Commander Wheaton strode toward him. The Commander was a big, beefy man, and his face was red with anger.

Stan snapped to attention.

"Sir, I—I'm sorry. I—"

"Just how do you explain disobeying my orders? Do you realize the trouble you're in? We've lost men because they flew poor formation. Are you trying to make the casualty list longer?"

"No, sir. I'm sorry, but I couldn't make myself close in. Not after what happened Monday."

It was out now.

Wheaton hesitated before answering.

"I'll give this more thought, Hunter, but you'll have to report to the screening board. If you can't carry out flight orders, you're a hazard to your squadron. I'll make the appointment for you. You'll be considered for elimination from the training program."

"Yes, sir," Stan murmured as the Commander hurried to the debriefing room. This was the end of his dream. Next week he'd be looking for a job, any job, around a space port.

Crushed with his own failure, Stan turned in his altitude gear for the last time. Slowly, he walked to the mess hall. He took sandwiches and coffee and plunked down near the end of the table where his flight mates were already eating a late lunch.

"Tell you what I was doing up there," Bill Almond was saying. "Well, I throttled back at seventy thousand and . . ."

His high-pitched voice went on, and the others seemed to be listening intently. Bill was a great spinner of space tales, mostly about himself, and usually nobody paid much attention. But now the other three space trainees hung on every bragging word as if he were a real hero.

Stan knew why. If they listened to Bill, they wouldn't have to speak to him. Leaving his food untouched, he shoved back his chair and walked out.

As he opened the barracks door, the base communications loudspeaker over his head rattled. A tense voice began reading orders in sharp, crisp tones.

"B Flight, attention. All pilots report to Operations. B Flight pilots report to the Operations Officer."

Stan's flight. He sat on his tightly made bunk; pictured his buddies scrambling from the mess hall, dashing to the Operations Building. But B Flight had been scheduled for a twenty-four-hour rest. Something was up. And here he was under orders to report for washout.

Stan hunched on the cot, staring at the varnished floor. The base was quiet under the early summer sunlight, yet he sensed excitement.

Thirty minutes later, the afternoon was shattered by the bark of jet engines firing one after another. Stan jumped to his feet. Certainly there was no training flight assigned. B Flight must have been assigned an actual mission!

He tried to relax and forget it. But that was no good. In ten minutes, he was pushing through the aluminum door of the Operations Center.

The Assignment Room was deserted, but he saw where the clerks had gone. A small crowd clustered in the doorway of the room marked Radar Tracking. Stan joined the hushed group and studied the large rectangular radar screen built into the wall at the far end of the radio-packed room.

On the left portion of the darkened screen, Stan spotted a group of greenish pinpoints of light. Slowly, they drifted toward the right, across the radar field.

"What is it?" he asked the clerk at his elbow.

The little assignment clerk answered without taking his eyes off the screen. "Meteor field. Drifting right into the inbound space lane. B Flight's gone after them."

Stan studied the tense faces around him. "What's all the worry for? We've had meteors in the space lanes before."

"The ore freighter on the moon run is flying an interception course with the meteor field."

"Oh-oh." Stan knew the freighter would be out of radio contact until the crew needed landing instructions. The freighters were tramp ships with no long range liaison radio sets.

"There's B Flight!" a voice cried.

They couldn't make it. The radar men saw that from the beginning. The meteors sizzled through the space lane, sucked in by gravity. The dots that were B Flight moved one third up the screen and no further. The SF-7s had reached their range limit, and the meteors drifted on.

"Increase your field," an officer snapped.

The pips on the radar screen seemed to grow smaller, but Stan realized the radar tracker had adjusted his range to take in a larger portion of space.

"There's the Alioth, high at center," the operator said. There was a flurry of whispers, then a hush fell over the room. The freighter sped unswerving into the meteor field.

The pinpoint of light was lost for a second, then reappeared flying a slightly different course.

"She's through!"

"But she's been hit. That course changed too fast."

"Her steering tubes," a quiet voice said. "She must be damaged; out of control. Gravity's pulling her in like a bomb. I'm afraid we'll have to stop her."

"No pilots," someone said. "They're all out on missions."

"Not all of them," Stan heard himself say. He shoved through the group, emerged in the murky radar room. Then he stiffened and saluted. The speaker with the quiet voice was the base commander, Richard Mason! His short-cropped gray hair was rumpled with worry.

"Your name, Airman?"

"Hunter, sir. Trainee Stanley Hunter."

"Trainee, eh? Well, Hunter, there's no time to

lose. I'll have an SF-7 prepared immediately. You're to intercept that freighter and find if it is disabled. If it is, order the crew to abandon ship at fifteen thousand feet, then shoot the freighter out of the air. We can't afford to take the chance of its hitting some town and blowing up."

If Stan had proved a poor pilot this morning, he wasn't going to be a poor airman now.

"Sir, I think you should know. I've been grounded by Commander Wheaton for disobeying orders this morning."

A silence hit the room. Then the Commander spoke. "Unofficially, I'm aware of that, Hunter. But it takes several hours for training notices to reach my office. I haven't seen any report on you yet, so officially I know nothing about that incident. My orders are to take off immediately."

Stan tried to hold back his grin, but it broke through.

"You're an honest pilot, anyway," the officer said. He held out his hand. "Good luck."

Half an hour later, at full throttle with the afterburner on, Stan's SF-7 roared through the thin air of the stratosphere. On his gyro compass, he held the heading given him by the radar astrogator which would intercept him with the Alioth four thousand miles out in space.

He turned off his jet drive and switched to full

rocket propulsion. He retracted the wings until only their outer third was visible.

The earth's curve became sharper. It wouldn't be long before he sighted the Alioth. Stan looked over his shoulder through the canopy and saw that night had fallen over the eastern United States, and darkness was extending west toward the long California coastline. Niagara was well into the evening.

"Hunter," the high intensity radio blared, "change your course to azimuth 047, elevation 087. Expect intercept in twenty-two minutes."

The astrogator back at Niagara was right. Just over twenty minutes later, Stan squinted against the brilliantly reflected sun from his silver cowling and stared ahead. A tiny aluminum tube suspended in space grew into the moon freighter, Alioth.

As she fell toward him, Stan saw the ship was disabled, all right. A deep meteor gash extended from amidships aft to the directional rocket drive. With these tubes out, the Alioth was a derelict.

Stan turned his ultra high frequency set to the commercial space frequency. "Freighter Alioth, this is Space Patrol. Over."

Scratchily, the Alioth answered. "This is Alioth. Go ahead."

"You are disabled by meteor collision. Is that roger?"

"That is roger, Space Patrol. We're drifting. Glad to have you along, but there's nothing you can do."

"What do you mean?" Stan asked. "My orders are to tell you to abandon ship at fifteen thousand."

"And you destroy the ship?" the Alioth radioman asked.

"Those are my orders."

The reply came slowly. "This is the Alioth's captain. We won't abandon ship. Five men hurt when the meteor hit. Shoot us down, but we won't bail out."

The man was in a shocked state, Stan realized. That made it tough. He could never shoot down a ship full of men, orders or no orders. But if they wouldn't bail out . . .

An amber instrument panel light flashed. He switched to the air-to-earth radio.

"Hunter, did you contact the Alioth?"

"Roger," Stan said. "They are derelict, but won't abandon ship—they have wounded aboard."

"Stand by."

There was a fifteen-second silence. "Hunter.

This is the base commander. What is your position?"

"Trailing the Alioth three miles behind."

"You'll have to destroy that freighter."

"Sir, I—"

"Orders, Hunter." Twenty men could not be spared to endanger hundreds. But Stan could not yet make himself accept the job. There must be another way. If he could only orbit a while; think it over—

Stan's brain hummed, hardly daring to accept his sudden idea. Orbit! That might be it. The Alioth might be able to orbit, circle the earth on centrifugal force like a miniature moon. A repair ship could get to her.

But how could it be done? The freighter was helpless with no directional power.

Then Stan's stomach tightened. He knew how to do it. *His* ship had directional power.

"Hunter," the radio demanded. "You'll be through the tropopause in ten minutes."

"Roger, sir. Will you stand by ten minutes?"

"Keep that ship from blowing up Chicago, and I will."

Stan drew a long breath. "Roger."

With fear he couldn't fight down, Stan opened his rocket valves and closed the distance between the ships. The Alioth was huge, a metal wall

ahead. Stan's hand trembled on the control stick; he was sweating, but he wouldn't turn back.

Side by side, the two craft hurtled toward earth. Slowly, Stan opened the climb valve. His patrol ship eased toward the Alioth. He could see the meteor pocks on the Alioth's hull. If he tangled in that gash—

Carefully, he inched on full power. The SF-7 neared the freighter until mere yards separated them. It was hard to believe they were traveling at thousands of miles per hour. The optical illusion made them appear to hang in space.

He drew in oxygen, held it. The SF-7 bumped the Alioth. Stan rammed the throttle open the rest of its travel, glued the patrol ship against the freighter with acceleration and stuck there.

In a long arc, the two craft swerved off their downward course and angled across the earth's surface. Then they paralleled. It had worked!

"Space Patrol to Alioth!" Stan shouted. "You're orbiting. I'll have a repair ship sent. Good luck."

The captain's voice was choked. "We don't know how to thank you."

"Roger, Alioth," Stan grinned. He shifted to ground frequency.

"Heard it all," Mason rapped. "You're in that

close." There was a pause. "When you land, there's a short course in understanding orders you ought to take."

"Yes, sir," Stan said.

"By the way, Hunter, Wheaton sends his congratulations."

Stan leaned back. He was tired and happy.

LOAD
OF
TROUBLE

by Edward W. Wood

I was sitting around in the Space Express offices, calculating how much longer I could hold out without getting another job, when the loudhailer blared. "Tim McGuire out there?" It was the agent.

"Yeah."

"In here, Tim. I've got a trip for you."

I was into the office but quick. "I'll take it," I told him as he looked up.

He laughed. "You're getting to the bottom of your sock, I can tell."

I sat on the edge of his desk. "You're not fooling, Pete." I was serious. The big companies could afford to run freight to Mars for exactly a hundred dollars a pound less than I could and I was losing customers all the time.

"Look, I don't care how dangerous this load is, I want it." I remembered the time I handled the delion, gruesome stuff. I was sick from the radiation for months after.

Pete looked at me and laughed; he shook with laughter. "Nothing you ever handled could come near this load for trouble."

My mouth was dry. "Where's the joke then?" I have to work but I don't enjoy risking my neck any more than the other guy.

Pete held his hands up for quiet. "You took a load to Alun once, remember, food pills and drugs for the Alunic sickness."

I nodded dumbly. I recall that one whenever I don't sleep; we had to stay quarantined in the ship for three weeks on our return so the sickness wouldn't take here on earth. It was a form of madness, but contagious. I cleared my throat harshly. "Alun is no joke, Pete, but I'll go. I hope it's a worthwhile load, not some minimum charge hoist."

He spread his hands. "This one is good, a ton and a quarter."

I whistled; my maximum payload is a ton and a half, but I had never been this near it before.

"What is it, more drugs and food?"

"Well," Pete began, "in a way it's both. You see, it's a live cow."

I laughed with him then. "You're fooling, Pete. You must be."

"No, this is deadly earnest. The foundation for space medicine believes it has a serum to beat Alunic sickness. I don't know too much about it, except it can't be transported frozen or in bottles, only alive in a cow." I nodded, understanding his point.

"You'll carry one of the foundation's veterinarians with you to attend to the animal," Pete added.

I stood up. "When do I start?"

"As soon as you can." Pete was looking through the papers in a file. "They want it immediately. I'm to provide you with the equipment at their expense and you'll be paid when you return." He wrote out two chits and handed them to me.

"Take this one to the fuel depot and get Katie ready, and this one to the space crewman's pool. Get yourself two good men. I'll see you tomorrow."

"Thanks, Pete." I folded the papers and put them into my pocket.

I went out scratching my head thoughtfully. This was funny. In this day of synthetic foods, the only cow I ever saw was in the zoo.

Down at the fuel yards I arranged for Katie to

be armed up with enough fuel. Katie is one of the original K87s that made the first trips back in the seventies. She was horribly inefficient, but a pretty reliable bus for all that. The fuel engineer is a buddy of mine.

"Got myself a load, Jack." I told him what it was and he laughed. Seems to me that everyone on earth laughed that day, but I didn't care, nor did the two men I hired. Jack Stewart, the engineer, said his folks had been farmers in the old days and he knew a little bit about animals. My communications man, Fred Bailey, knew as much as I did. This was going to be a headache.

At nine the next morning we were sitting round Pete's desk discussing details. The cowman from Spacemed was there, an earnest kind of guy wearing old-fashioned spectacles. We listened while he outlined the problems. I don't think he had done very much space travel, but he sure knew lots about his cow.

"I have checked a scale model of your machine," he told me, "and I find that your freight holds will not accommodate a cow. However, I have made plans for the animal to travel in the control cabin."

My two crewmen looked at one another in dismay, but I just shrugged. Even if I would have to step around a cow, I still needed this job.

"There's no spare room in the cabin," I reminded him. "Ah!" he began eagerly. "Let me explain." So we just listened. After all it was his party. When he had finished, I could think of nothing to add so we left, to reassemble next morning at the ship.

I was there four hours ahead of time, but the others joined me soon after. We did our checks, all the routine ground testing. Then the doc arrived, bringing his protégé. She looked harmless enough, a big brown and white beast, staring about amiably. The gangplank was put up, and we started easing her in through the crew door. All the old K87s had the big doors, to allow for the cumbersome spacesuits of those days; none of the modern ships would have got the animal in their doors. That's why I had the load.

The doc backed in first holding a bundle of cow food, and she followed him in peacefully. My two crewmen fastened the nylon acceleration straps under her belly and we all heaved her up tight against the ceiling. That did it. She bawled till our ears rang. There was about three feet of space under the cow's feet and we scrambled out from under her.

"How do I see my gauges, chief?" Stewart wanted to know when we were outside. "That darn cow is right over the monitor."

"You'll have to do the best you can," I told him irritably. "Look, Doc, can't you give that thing a needle to keep it quiet?"

"Oh, no!" He was aghast. "It would induce a state of depression injurious to the serum. I'm afraid we must put up with the noise."

"Okay, okay." I moved away. I had to recheck my gear before we started. At fifteen minutes before launching, we were locked in and ready. Stewart was checking his clocks, slowly going round each one visually. Bailey was tinkering with the radar beam directional gear and the doc was milking the cow. Imagine, kneeling carefully between her feet, milking her into a bucket on the floor.

"How often do we have this caper?" I asked him.

He looked at me, very seriously. "Every twelve hours, Captain. I have a mechanical contrivance which I shall use when we are underway."

"Good. Are you sure you've got everything else you need?"

He pushed the bucket clear, crawled out from under the cow, and stood up. "Yes, I have her space equipment stowed in the hold."

"Okay, Doc, put that milk away and take up position." I liked this little man. He had no thought in his head except for the welfare of his charge. I like to see a man as conscientious as that.

He scuttled down the companionway with his bucket and was up a minute later buckling himself into his harness on the wall. The rest of us were strapped in by now, resting under the spring tension up against the deckhead.

The cow had extra straps around her jaw to level out the pressure; it had stopped her bawling, too, thanks be. At L-hour the lights glowed and I threw the switches. For perhaps a second we paused, and then in ferocious acceleration we began to sag downwards in our G-harness. The cow was facing me. I saw her eyes grow bigger in astonishment as we moved slowly down the wall. Just as her feet touched the deck, the ship began to steady and she was drawn up again like a big clumsy yoyo.

Then we were free of gravity. I unsnapped my harness and felt my way down the wall to the floor, clamping my space shoes firmly down. The doc was uncoupled before me. Trudging awkwardly on his clamp shoes over to the cow, he undid her chin strap and started to tap her chest with a stethoscope. She looked at him curiously, swishing her tail slowly from side to side.

Without looking up, the doc patted her on the neck. "She is in grand shape, Captain," he told me. "Heart completely normal."

"That's good." I was setting the controls to cruising conditions, settling down for the twenty-six-hour trip.

Stewart touched my sleeve. "I'm afraid I won't get my first check completed unless I can use the monitor. Can we move the cow for a while?"

"I guess you'd better ask Doc," I told him.

Doc looked thoughtful for a moment; then he said, "I don't see why not. I don't think it would harm her now."

Stewart and I unfastened the straps. Then Doc gave the cow a little push and she sailed away across the ceiling like a toy balloon at a children's party. Stewart tuned the monitor and began making rapid notes on his log. I was watching the cow. She gave out a loud horrified lowing and the force of it drove her backwards through the air. She cannoned off Stewart's head and began to bounce about between the walls, bawling. It was too much for me. I laughed till the tears ran. Bailey and the doc were trying to catch hold of her. Doc was in a panic.

"Captain, this is making her nervous."

"Okay." I clumped over and took her by the horns. Doc was making a leash for her, out of the chin stay. He lashed it round a stanchion and passed the end round her horns. She hovered there, an angry captive balloon.

Doc said, "We must refasten her as soon as possible." He was pale with the worry.

"Take it easy, Doc. She'll be fine now."

I went back to my computer, leaving him patting her neck soothingly. The next second he was shouting again. Turning, I saw the cow upside down, her feet waving wildly. The doc was trying to turn her rightside up, but the strap had caught and she was stuck head down. I took a deep breath, counted ten, and unfastened the strap from her horns. Then I pushed her foot. She revolved twice and finished off upright.

"Stewart," I said, ignoring the doctor, "for Pete's sake, hurry with your checks before I go berserk."

"Roger, Captain." He clicked off the monitor and we hauled the animal up into place again. She seemed to feel at home there because she stopped bawling and just looked us over coldly.

She stayed there for the next two watches. I was below when Doc milked her, but I came on watch in time for another game of handball when Stewart made his midtrip checks. This time we held on to her until it was over. Then I took control. I managed quite well, despite having to go on hands and knees every time I wanted to cross the cabin. At least I did manage until Doc appeared up the companionway with an armful

of dry grass. I was on the other side of the cow. Suddenly my settings altered and the ship began to accelerate alarmingly. I hailed Stewart and he came up the ladder at a run. I heard him blistering the doctor.

Then his head poked through and he said briefly, "Doc was using the rocket controls as a feed rack, and the cow pulled our boosters on."

I slapped my forehead. "He sure is in the right business. He's a farm boy all through."

Stewart went back below and Doc crawled in. "Sorry, Captain, I was carried away."

"You should be," I told him grinning. "What's the problem now?"

"I wonder if you would help me give her a drink." We had to unfasten her. I held her while she sucked up the water and we lashed her up again without incident. I began to feel kindly disposed towards her.

"What will they do with her, Doc? They won't slaughter her, will they?"

"Oh, no," he told me. "She will be used as an incubator for the serum." He gave her a prod. "You observe that it produces no ill effects."

I was glad of that. I was becoming attached to that cow. I went below and opened the fridge. It was full of cattle food, greens, and little bales of grass. All the crew supplies had been put on one of the shelves underneath; everything was warm and horrible. I drank my lukewarm water. The passenger's comfort came first aboard Katie.

It was at the next milking that the accident happened. The doc had his electric milker plugged in and the cow was swishing her tail from side to side contentedly when there was a flash and all the lights on the non-vital circuit went out. Stewart hastily checked the fuse boxes. "They're burnt out," he informed me.

"Emergency power on," I ordered. The lights came on and we saw the cow stretched out stiffly. The doctor quickly checked her heart and lungs.

"That's strange," he said, straightening up. "Her involuntary muscles are working, heart and lungs normal, but all voluntary function has ceased." He shook his head. "It is, without doubt, some form of electrocution."

Then Bailey spoke, "All the ground directional gear is out of function, Captain." He was a quiet man. I guessed it must be permanent trouble or he would not have reported it.

"Can you fix it?"

"No, the tubes are dead." He smiled. "Makes an expensive glass of milk, doesn't it?"

I nodded briefly. "You've got two hours before we enter the gravity pull of Alun. Do your best."

We would need that gear to find our way up

the radar beam to Alun's landing area. It was no use crossing the universe with a cow and then dropping it off in one of the vast deserts that covered Alun. We had to home on to the city where the Spacemed outpost was situated.

The doc was on his knees under the cow for the rest of the trip. "She will be all right when this coma passes," he said. "I don't think the serum will be harmed."

Well, that was the big thing. I left him beside the cow, even though he was in the way.

Soon we felt the first touch of gravity from Alun. I had Bailey watch the telescreen, checking what passed under our emergency scanner. After a trip completely round the planet, he reported: "It's no use, Captain. I'll have another try at the beam gear."

I nodded shortly. Things were bad. We did not have enough fuel to circle indefinitely, yet if we put the doc down in the desert, both he and the cow would die. I didn't want that on my conscience. That cow had me beat.

I laughed. "Modern science beaten by a cow. They got around for centuries on their own feet."

But Doc was not listening to me. He undid the straps that fastened the cow. Drawn by gravity, she flopped against the side of the ship. He hoisted her up clear of the floor by the center strap.

"Look," he said. "Her tail! She's magnetic." Her tail was out stiff, indicating the beam, and her whole body swung very slowly.

"Turn right," he told me.

I pushed the air drag that side. As we watched, the cow swung around until her tail was pointing in the same direction as before. Without another word, I turned the ship until we were running in the direction the cow was pointing. I put on all the drag we could bear and we ran slowly around Alun at about eight hundred knots. My throat was dry. I knew we had fuel for only one run. Then the cow began to dip her tail down towards the ground. I brought the ship up vertically and slackened off. The cow began to turn over and then wedged in her strap. Slowly I brought the ship down. The radio altimeter was useless and I had to depend on the oblique facing scanner to give an idea of altitude. We landed with a smash that jarred the whole frame of the ship.

Bailey said, "She's moving."

The cow suddenly went limp.

Then the radio began to blare. "Do you receive me? Your location please, K87. Do you read me?"

I answered, "K87 to Alun control, we are down; believe within monitoring distance of you."

The voice came back. "We have you fixed now, 87. Are you okay?"

I handed the transmitter to Bailey. "Tell them about it all; tell them how we used a cow for a compass. I have to dress the lady."

I helped the doctor swathe the cow in her suit. It was a complicated affair with a great many straps and we sweated a lot doing it. When she was bound and had her oxygen mask in place, she was wedged tightly in the cabin.

Doc dressed slowly; he was thinking hard. "It was all a matter of static electricity, that was why the radio started again."

"That's right, Doc." I was sorry to be leaving him on this miserable planet, but it was his work. "Maybe you can patent the idea."

Bailey came back to me, "There's a party outside now, skipper. Is Doc ready?"

I turned to the doc. "Are you fit?"

"Yes, I'm ready now, Captain."

"Okay, open the inner door."

The three of us crewmen pushed the cow into the space lock. It was a tussle.

Then Doc shook hands all round. "Thanks for the ride," he said to me.

I thumped his shoulder affectionately. "Thanks for the experience, Doc, and good luck."

We shut the door and he released himself from

the space lock. Through the camera we saw the last of him. He was bounding after the cow, which was taking twenty-foot leaps into the air.

Stewart said, "Heck, I meant to remind him about the gravity here."

"Never mind," I said, as we prepared to take off again. "Doc won't mind, but you should have warned his cow."

BEST FRIEND

by A. M. Lightner

Dr. Hercules Valla, eminent scientist, made the final adjustments to the electrodes and let his hand linger affectionately upon Candy's woolly head.

"Good dog," he said softly, mindful of the fact that some of the other people working in the shed might think it odd to hear a man of his standing talking to his experimental animal.

Candy's tongue licked Dr. Valla's hand. She lay relaxed upon her foam rubber shock absorber and watched him with loving, trustful eyes.

"Everything's going to be fine," he muttered, scratching her ears and smoothing down her tail under the harness. "In a few hours you'll be back with us, and this time it's for keeps. You're being retired to house pet, Candy. We'll get you a husband and you can have your pups on my bed."

Candy licked him again and Valla hastily withdrew his hand and snapped the plastic dome into place, while sternly repressing the feelings of reluctance and dread that invariably assailed him at this point.

"She's all yours," he said to the waiting mechanics, and walked off without stopping to watch them fit the capsule into the waiting nose cone.

Outside he met his friend, the mathematician, Dr. Milton Rowan. The younger man fell into step beside him.

"Got Candy all trussed up?" he asked. "Said a fond farewell? You want to watch that talking to your animals! Next thing to talking to yourself."

"She needs a morale booster like anyone else. I'd like to see you take off on this joy ride without even a kiss from your wife."

"If I intended to ride a rocket, I'd keep my wife as far away as possible. Glad I didn't go into that end of the business! Don't you think it's a little underhanded to tell the poor pooch that everything's going to be fine, when you know any of a dozen disasters is possible?"

Dr. Valla shuddered. "It isn't reassurance she needs. It's love and my approval. You can't train an animal without that. And I wouldn't be doing this work if I didn't know there's going to be a man riding that thing soon."

"Yes, they've got the bugs pretty well ironed out," said Rowan. "I don't think you need worry about Candy—much. Where are you planning to watch it?"

"The boat's leaving any minute. Got to get down range where they expect to pick her up." He stopped to fumble in his pockets and withdrew a small, oblong box. "Candy wouldn't forgive me if I turned up without these."

Dr. Rowan squinted at the yellow package labeled "Canine Yum-Yums."

"You'll never learn not to get emotionally involved with your experiment! Well, I've got to get back to my computers. I'll see you when it's over."

The countdown proceeded without a hitch. The launching was successful, and as the vehicle roared skyward, Dr. Rowan found himself muttering "Lucky dog!" and then smiling as he thought of his friend, speeding across the ocean toward a rendezvous at a time and place calculated by his machines.

"Good thing she didn't blow," he said to a watching scientist. "I believe it'd break Valla's heart if anything happened to that dog now. It's the third time she's been up and she's due for retirement. Funny how some men let themselves get involved with their tools of trade."

"Don't kid yourself," said the other. "How'd you feel if someone or something smashed up that computer of yours?"

The very thought made Rowan stutter. "Why, I . . . I . . . that would be criminal! And besides it isn't a risk of the experiment."

"At least you could rebuild the computer," said the man.

At this point the work of that instrument claimed Dr. Rowan's attention and he had no time to think of a fitting reply. The signals from the rocket had to be fed into the machine, together with the reports of sightings as they came in. The orbit had to be figured and the points of re-entry and landing sent to the distant ship. Dr. Rowan was absorbed with details and only later did an ugly fact begin to dawn upon him. The rocket was not in the proper orbit.

"Tell them to hurry up and eject that capsule," he ordered, "or it's going to be too late."

He continued to work with the computer, and not till well along in the morning was he finally convinced of his results. Then he sat back to relax and glanced up at the military man leaning over his shoulder.

"Well, did you eject?" he snapped.

The man shook his head. "The mechanism failed to work. And it seems to be too far away now. When do you figure it'll be back again?"

Rowan experienced a sinking sensation. "That thing isn't coming back," he said. "Not for a long time. It's headed out beyond Jupiter."

He threw down his pencil in annoyance. Why should he feel this way? It was only a dog—not a man. But he kept seeing Hercules Valla, standing on a pitching deck with a box of Canine Yum-Yums in his hand.

The satellite raced on into outer space. Candy lay in her little nest and drowsed. For that is what dogs do when waiting for their master. The unpleasant acceleration, which she had learned to expect at the beginning of a flight, was over. She was not unduly troubled by the feeling of weightlessness, for she was held by the straps of her harness. The electrodes sent back to earth the record of her breathing and her heartbeat until the distance became too great for the tiny radio to span. Candy slept, her ears ever alert for the click of the capsule's opening to tell her that her master was there.

In the far reaches of the solar system the satellite was a meteor, hurtling along with its own

thrust, its orbit determined by the pull of the celes-
tial bodies that it passed. But space is infinite com-
pared with earth. The billions of suns and their
attendant planets harbor many wonders. And on
a little moon of an outer planet, two such wonders
were sitting when Candy's vehicle shot past.

Kondar and Zylph had been scouting the
galaxy and paused to rest and set up their instruments on this convenient island in space. They
knew that habitable planets are few and far between, and the chance of finding one with intelligent life even less likely. But intelligent life at the
same point of development as their race—beings
who could talk sensibly, act cooperatively and
generally communicate on the same level of understanding—that had never been found in the
ten thousand years that their people had been at
large in the galaxy.

Kondar was adjusting an instrument much like
the telescope, while Zylph busied himself with
setting up a temporary dwelling. Kondar called
to his friend.

"There's something interesting here. Come and
take a look. Too big to be a meteor. Too small to
be a moon of any sort. And besides it looks
peculiar."

Zylph obliged by squinting through the instrument.

"Definitely not natural," he declared. "Hurry up and catch it before it gets away."

Since their space ship was far, far in advance of anything dreamed of on earth, it took Kondar only a short time to catch up with the satellite and bring it back to the little moon. Zylph had the temporary headquarters ready. The nose cone was set down; the lid was pried off; and the two galactic beings stared at Candy and her trappings.

"It's unbelievable!" cried Kondar. "Intelligent life in this unlikely spot!"

"It looks rather dead," said Zylph. "And it's all strapped up. It couldn't be piloting the vessel in that condition."

"Not intelligent," guessed Kondar. "No hands, you see. Probably a lower form sent as an experiment. You realize what this means, Zylph! There must be intelligent beings back where this came from, and they're just beginning to learn about space flight."

"And we discovered them!" sighed Zylph. "On our first hundredth trip!"

"Well, let's examine it! Get the revitalizer and the translator. Get the thought analyzer. We mustn't miss our big chance!"

So Candy was revitalized. She was taken out of her cocoon and fed and watered and treated with the utmost care. She didn't like the smell of

the strange people who let her out of her cage, but she was a tractable animal. She had learned to accept many peculiar things. She ate and drank what was offered and submitted when more machines and electrodes were fixed upon her. But all the time she was wishing that Dr. Valla would come and put an end to this foolishness. On every previous flight the door of the cage had been opened by her beloved master proffering candy, and she had no doubt that in the fullness of time he would appear.

The translator quickly demonstrated that dogs do not speak or have a language. But Kondar was not discouraged. He merely switched on the "brain analyzer." This remarkable machine could take thought pictures and emotions directly from the brain waves of the subject, and from it Kondar and Zylph received their first impression of the planet Earth.

They quickly realized that Kondar's guess had been correct. The masters of the planet, seen through the eyes of this animal, were very intelligent and remarkable creatures. Practically gods of their world.

But it was more than that. As the "analyzer" was turned up, the two aliens were suffused with a surging blast of love.

"Did you feel that?" asked Zylph in an awed whisper.

"Almost knocked me down," agreed Kondar.

"But don't you realize," chattered Zylph, his excitement rising, "any people able to inspire love like that in the lower animals must be wonderful!"

"And we know that they've reached a high technical level. They're about to burst out into the galaxy. Zylph, my friend, we've found what everyone's dreamed of since we first hit space!"

"A brother planet," breathed Zylph. "A species to share the galaxy with! Do you think we can find where this thing came from?"

"Must be one of the inner planets in this system. All we have to do is go in and look. You and I are going to be famous!"

The two aliens gathered up their gear, dismantled their shelter, and packed everything, including Candy and her capsule, into their space ship.

By the time they reached the orbit of Jupiter it was evident that they were headed in the right direction. In spite of the electronic noise coming from the giant planet, their sensitive instruments were able to pick up radio signals that could only be made by intelligent beings. By the time they hit the orbit of Mars, it was coming in clearly and they were receiving the voices of the strangers. They hooked up their translating machine and proceeded to a landing on the third planet's moon.

So Kondar and Zylph listened to a sampling of an ordinary night's radio, and their first impulse to make quick contact with the new world was arrested. The music was an uproar to their ears. The advertising made no sense. But it was the news that overwhelmed them.

A frenzied voice told of gang warfare in the big cities, of murder in Texas and kidnapping in Iowa. It described a new "anti-matter" bomb and gave an account of renewed bloodshed in Africa. It ended with a report on the peace talks in Geneva, where another snag had developed.

At this point, Kondar reached out and switched off the translator. The voice went on yammering in the same foreign tongue, but it was a relief not to be able to understand it.

"There seems to be something wrong somewhere."

Zylph nodded miserably. "Only just this side of barbarism. We were fools to think we could beat the Old Ones at this game."

"But the animal," Kondar protested. "There was no mistake about that. We both felt it. How could an animal like this—intelligent as such creatures go—feel this blind, adoring love for these . . . these . . . ?"

"I know," said Zylph sadly. "There must be something there. Something we've missed. Perhaps in ten thousand years . . ."

"When we are dust. That's always the way. We're either too early or too late. Well, we'd better clear out before one of them spots us. If they're beginning to have space travel, we don't want them to follow us home. In their present state they won't be fit to live with."

Zylph agreed, but as they prepared to take off for the second time, they were startled by the strange behavior of the animal. Candy had risen to her feet with her eyes on the instrument "speaker" where a new voice from the planet was being piped into the ship. Her ears were cocked, her tail was up. She gave voice to a soft whine that started low down and rose in intensity till it erupted in a series of quick, eager barks. Soon she was running about the cabin, searching for the voice and crying pathetically. Then she lay down as near the source of the sound as possible, while a low moan came from her throat, the essence of loneliness and despair.

Kondar switched on the translator and a different voice came over. "You have just heard Dr. Hercules Valla, speaking for better international friendship and agreement to ban atomic testing. Dr. Valla is with the space-flight program being carried on in our state and we are fortunate to have him tonight as a guest. Our next speaker will be . . ."

A third voice took over, but Candy had lost interest. Zylph switched off the receiver and they both stared at the animal. The two aliens vividly remembered those pulsing waves of love.

"What are we going to do with this creature?" Kondar voiced the thought that was troubling them both.

"It's a pity to take her away. She wouldn't be happy with us."

"You know the rules. We must leave no trace of our visit."

"But that voice was the man she loves. Can't we send her back to him?"

"Don't be foolish. How could she find him in a whole world? And could we do it without their knowing?"

"We still have her harness and parachute. We could take her down most of the way. The voice was coming from that long spit of land. I could almost pinpoint it."

"Well, it's against all the regulations. But there never was a case quite like this. Get the harness on her while I take us down."

Hercules Valla and Milton Rowan were going home after the lecture. Dr. Rowan had insisted on driving his friend, for you could never be sure, under the circumstances, whether he had his mind on what he was doing.

It was a beautiful moonlit night and by common consent they stopped along a deserted beach to enjoy the peace and beauty of the ocean. Ever since the last shoot, Dr. Valla had been silent and withdrawn, and Rowan was worried by his friend's despondent mood. And so he was relieved when the doctor began to speak.

"Look at her up there," said Hercules Valla, pointing at the moon. "What won't Man do to get there! How much money have we squandered already! How many innocent animals have been sacrificed and how many men will be! But one day soon we'll get there. It will be either we or the Russians."

"Yes, they may put men on the moon any day now."

"Well, I hope their ejection system works better than poor Candy's. I hope. . . ."

He stopped and Rowan had the uncomfortable feeling that the soft-hearted scientist was going to cry. He searched his brain frantically for something cheerful to say. Something to make the failure sound like success, to make Candy's sacrifice constructive. He was about to come out with some ill-chosen words when Valla held up a hand and Rowan realized that he was listening intently.

"Don't you hear it?" asked Dr. Valla. "There's a dog barking."

Now he's really off his rocker, thought Rowan, but he only said, "I don't hear anything."

"You've been listening to your old machine for so long that you're getting deaf." And Dr. Valla began to whistle in a high, peculiar way.

Rowan became alarmed. If this weren't his best friend, he'd certainly describe the fellow as batty. Valla surely had been overworking. He'd better get him to a doctor when he got back to the base.

And then inconceivably there was a noise in the bushes. A rushing, a scrabbling, accompanied by a high-pitched whining, and a small dog burst from the underbrush and threw itself upon Dr. Valla. In the uncertain moonlight, assisted by the glare from the headlights, Dr. Rowan saw that it did look very much like Herc's experimental animal. Its back was marked with the same dark patches, and its tail vibrated with all the frantic excitement of a one-man dog that has been separated too long from its master. Dr. Rowan wondered if he was losing his mind, too.

"Now get hold of yourself, Valla," he cautioned. "This thing's upset you so that every friendly dog you meet in the bush sets you thinking about Candy."

"But it *is* Candy!" cried Dr. Valla. "Can't you see? Can't you hear her?" He picked the dog up to let it lick his face, and went off into a string of endearments that were nauseating to Rowan.

"Now look here, Valla. The dog may look like Candy and it may sound like Candy—but it can't *be* Candy. You mustn't let yourself be carried away by these fantasies. I've been warning you to keep a hold on reality."

"Oh, is that so!" said Dr. Valla sharply. "I guess I should know my own animal."

Rowan could see that this was going to be quite a problem, and he cursed himself for having agreed to stop and look at the moon.

"Be reasonable," he argued. "If that's Candy, how did she get here? You know we plotted her orbit out beyond Jupiter."

"That's easy," said Dr. Valla. "Your plottings were wrong. The capsule made a smaller orbit and came around and landed somewhere near here, where it wasn't expected."

"But that's quite impossible! It was picked up by all the tracking stations. In fact, we had radio contact for a good part of the distance. And it was all worked out and verified by my computer."

"All I can say is that your computer was wrong."

Rowan sputtered at the insult. "Wrong! My computer wrong! Do you realize what you're saying?"

"Yes, wrong. Blew a fuse, split a gasket, or whatever it is computers do."

"But that's impossible. If anything goes wrong, it gives a signal. And nothing has gone wrong. It's worked perfectly since then. It figured the orbits for the next shoot."

"Well, you'd better refigure them then. There's liable to be all kinds of errors."

Rowan shuddered at the mere possiblity. He drew himself up to reply.

"My computer," he said, "has never been wrong. I might be wrong—but not the computer. And you'd better get hold of yourself, man. How will this sound to the scientists at the base? Too much brooding over a lost pet. All too easy to mistake the first friendly stray."

Dr. Valla stopped scratching Candy's ears. "If I were on a desert island," he said, "or the surface of the moon, and you appeared unexpectedly, covered with dirt and unshaven, I would still know it was you. Because I know you. You're my friend. I could never mistake you no matter how peculiar or inexplicable the circumstances. And I could not mistake Candy. This is Candy."

The dog pricked up her ears at the name and whined ecstatically. Valla carried her to the car lights.

"Look here, if you have to have proof. Look at the marks of the harness. She must have squeezed out of it somehow. And here, feel under her coat. A part of the harness is still there!"

Against his will, Dr. Rowan felt. As he brushed the fur, the dog gave a low growl and her head whipped around with bared fangs. Rowan jerked back, but not before his fingers knew the truth of Valla's statement.

The professor laughed. "She never did like you, did she? Must sense that you prefer your machines."

Dr. Rowan remembered other occasions when Candy had snapped at him, and his mind tottered on the abyss.

"If it's true, where's the capsule?"

"I don't suppose we'll ever find that. But if we search the neighborhood in the morning, we ought to find the parachute."

Dr. Rowan did not answer. His mind was hastily turning over all the possibilities about the faulty computer. What could be the matter with it? Something terrible. Irreparable. He felt his life work crumbling, and made his way blindly to the car.

"Where are you going?" asked Dr. Valla.

"Got to get back and look at my computer. Got to figure this out."

"Good idea," said Valla. "But don't let it get you down. We have to keep a good hold on reality these days."

Rowan's reply was to rev the motor, so Valla climbed in beside him and held the door open.

"Hop in, Candy," he said. "We're going home."

THE TERRIBLE INTRUDERS

by James V. Hinrichs

Sol watched as Sol, the sun, rose. It was a play on words which Sol enjoyed. His well-known nickname (so well-known, in fact, that no one could remember his actual given name) had been the point of many good jokes—and many bad puns.

The true source of his nickname was lost in antiquity. The name had followed him to this desert, and he was known by no other. His friends, and he had many, said Sol suited him because he was a "sun worshiper." A few others, chuckling at their cleverness, said that he was called Sol because of his *sol*-itary confinement.

Both reasons were correct. Sol loved the sun; he could never get enough of its warmth. Indeed, that was the reason for his coming to this desert.

That, and his intense desire to own a piece of land. The other reason was correct also, because Sol did live alone. He had never minded being a "loner." In fact, he enjoyed it.

But in spite of his individuality, he was as well-liked as he was well-known. Everyone in the area was fond of Sol, the good-natured farmer who lived alone north of Pumping Station Fourteen.

He stood on top of the sand dune, with a feeling of quiet pride, looking down upon his farmland. The farm which he and a few machines had carved from the desert.

The cool, arid air of the desert morning refreshed Sol as he reflected upon the marvel which had made it all possible. It was the miracle of water. Water which had transformed a dying desert into a life-producing farm. Water, brought by gigantic canals, pumped by atomic engines.

Ah, yes, the atomic engines of this Atomic Age. Here it was 253 Atomic Age, and in those two and one-half centuries the people of this ancient planet had made more progress than in any other comparable era. Now the world was really bursting with life, and Sol was proud to have helped it.

He had come in—let's see, in '28, no, it was in the spring of '29—and in those twenty-four years

Sol had made more advancement than ever before. He had been a laborer, but now, now he was a farmer and a successful one, too.

So as Sol shuffled slowly over to his FJ (Flying Jeep, vintage 246 A.A.), it was not without some right that he boasted to himself: "Of course I'm proud of myself. Why shouldn't I be?"

But enough of this daydreaming, Sol scolded himself. "I'd better hop over to the north section and check that pump. The crops there aren't getting enough water and if I don't fix it, I'll lose the whole section."

A feeder line from the main power plant had been broken by some desert animal and Sol didn't discover it until he made his rounds four days later. Even in that short interval the desert had begun to reclaim its land. Without a continuous supply of life-sustaining water, the fertile soil begins to dry up and return to its previous dormant condition. The desert sands from adjoining, untilled acres begin to sift across the green crops and choke the life from the vital plants. Even four days without water could mean the difference between life and death, success and failure, at least in that portion of Sol's farm.

Sol's mind was so intent upon his problem that he didn't notice anything unusual until his FJ skimmed over the W-shaped sand dune. As Sol's eyes scanned the familiar horizon, he spotted a peculiar sparkle to the northwest.

"I haven't any time to spare," he thought, "but maybe I should check it. It might be another weather balloon—" he had found one a few months before "—and, after all, the reward money never hurts."

At the thought of the possible extra income, Sol had made his decision and the FJ was already winging toward the faint glitter. But even before Sol was halfway there, he knew that it couldn't be a weather balloon. It wasn't the dull glimmer of a small plastic balloon, but more the brilliant sparkle of . . . of . . . *metal!*

"That's impossible! With metal so scarce, the government would never waste any," he thought wonderingly.

Before Sol could come to a satisfactory answer, he was approaching the—as he could now dimly see—metal structure. For reasons Sol could not have explained, he was extremely cautious in approaching the mysterious object. So cautious, in fact, that he set the FJ down on the side of a nearby dune and slowly crawled up the side of the ridge.

Sol warily peeked over the edge of the powdery hill and let out an audible gasp of astonishment.

It was a *flying saucer!* Sol gazed in wonderment at the silver-colored, metallic disk. *Why would it be made of metal? All of our aircraft are plastic nowadays, since metal is so scarce.* He fought back the sinister thought that was creeping out of the dark reaches of his subconscious mind.

Sol turned and retreated down the slope a short distance. He leaned back and began to collect his thoughts about this strange intruder. For once, he was sorry that he lived alone. He would have been greatly comforted by the presence of a companion in this situation.

Sol remembered the flying saucer scare of 245 A.A. The government had passed it off as mass hallucination, figments of people's imaginations, experimental aircraft, weather balloons, and a host of other things. *This may be an experimental airplane, but it certainly isn't any figment of my imagination!* Apprehensively, he crawled up the embankment again to check. *Yes, it's still there. And . . . and now . . . there's . . . there's a door open!*

As Sol watched, appalled, three creatures so alien that they made him sick with fear, climbed out of the open hatch. His overwhelming dread of those lurid creatures so possessed him that he suffered a quaking he couldn't control.

Those . . . those creatures! Ugh! They're so horrible and revolting! I've . . . I've got to tell someone—anyone!

Maybe we're being invaded by those . . . those . . . those beasts!

Slowly, Sol began to gain a small measure of control over himself. The thought of possible capture by these intruders and its dire consequences had filtered into his panic-stricken mind. His consternation at this added terror prompted immediate action, and he started clambering down the sand dune all the while blubbering: *I've . . . I've got to warn everybody before those hideous two-legged creatures destroy me.* The purplish-green, six-legged, local resident continued slithering down the ridge. *I can't understand it. What on Mars is going on!*

THE SAMARITAN

by Richard Harper

The ship was in deep space, traveling with sleek mechanical precision at nearly the speed of light, its computers and drives all functioning automatically, moving it along a pre-determined course toward a certain planet of a certain star still four light years away.

Cmdr. Max Landin had the conn watch. Strapped in the deep cushioned chair of the control room, he monitored the maze of instruments set in banks around him while Edward Haverson, his watch officer, prepared a food compound in the starboard cubicle. William Berger, the watch medic, was busy in the aft-compartment giving the weekly sustenance injections to the other three crew members, the relief watch, who were sleeping soundly in a state of suspended animation.

A week of monitoring the course and actions of the ship, then three weeks of sleep, like a long weekend. Six light years had passed since leaving Earth, although for them the passing of time was only a few months, and they were right on schedule with no complications and everything going according to plan.

Yet they were beginning to feel the remoteness of their situation, the complete and utter isolation that was sometimes frightening. Max had noticed the strain first in Haverson, who was beginning to worry about things, little things like whether he was getting enough nourishment, or too much exercise. Medic Berger had assured him that all was in order, but even Berger was showing the effects of the awesomeness of prolonged flight.

In spite of being picked for special space aptitudes and trained for years in flights to the moon and Mars, a man never seemed to get used to the uncanny detached feeling of complete aloneness. And now for the first time man was venturing beyond Earth's solar system, reaching into infinity toward an unseen goal that existed only on their instruments.

A buzzer sounded on the console and moments

later Ed Haverson pulled himself into the compartment to relieve Landin. Giving over the conn of the ship, Max floated back along the passageway to his quarters, where he strapped himself in his bunk for a few hours' sleep. But he lay there, sleepless, thinking about his life and this ship and this flight, wondering what they were really doing a million miles from nowhere like a bubble on an endless sea? What were they really looking for? What did they expect to find?

Back on Earth he had looked up at the dark void on starlit nights and dreamed his dreams. And later on, after years of preparation and training, he'd been among the first crews to orbit the earth. What a small insignificant thing it seemed now, but what a fantastic adventure it had been then; the experimental trips to the moon and Mars that had followed; the ships and crews that had gone out and never returned. Space conquest was his life; but he was beginning to wonder if it was all worth it.

He dozed fitfully, and awakened startled at the sound of his name over the intercom. Haverson was calling him forward to the control room.

He found his watch officer busy checking and rechecking the instrument data and finding the readings hard to believe. Haverson unstrapped himself from the chair and let Max slide in while he hovered near his shoulder. "You check it out, skipper. I don't trust my readings."

Max Landin's hands moved over the console, deciphering, monitoring the information. He let out a slow breath. There was no mistake. The instruments were registering a large mass, evidently an asteroid. But what was incredible to them both was that the mass was sending out a signal, a constant beamed signal that was registering on the ship's instruments.

Ed Haverson was frowning. "Then I wasn't wrong? The instruments aren't malfunctioning?"

Max shook his head slowly. "No, you weren't wrong. The instruments aren't wrong."

"But, skipper, what—"

"Call Will up here," Max said quietly. He was thinking now, thinking hard. Everything had been so routinely simple that he hadn't realized how lax his thinking had become, but now whatever it was that was happening needed a calm, clear head.

William Berger pulled himself into the control room and clamped on beside Max. "What is it?"

Max handed him the data book and Berger, after studying it a moment, stared at the signal on the scope, fascinated. He looked at his commander. "And it checks out? It's a bona-fide signal, not some freak of space?"

"It checks out," Max Landin said.

"But—who's sending it?"

The question hung there in the air. The hiss of the ventilators seemed loud in the stillness.

Seconds later the signal was coming in stronger than ever and Max knew the time had come for a decision which the ship's instruments could not make. And the decision was his alone. As commander of the watch he had complete jurisdiction over the ship; but altering course was something planned only in case of an emergency, and as near as he could tell, the ship was in no danger. He could simply stay on course and ignore the signal. He had no authorization for landing anywhere short of their fixed goal, even for a little while. It could lead to any number of complications; it meant risking the ship, the personnel, the entire expedition. And according to all their data, they were nowhere. No nearby star system, no conceivable planet, only a barren lump of matter in an empty void. Yet there was no denying the signal. He had double-checked everything.

His curiosity alone was almost overwhelming, but curiosity couldn't be the basis for a decision; a decision he would have to make soon or they would be out of range. Already the signal had grown noticeably weaker. He looked at Haverson and Berger. They waited, watching him, and there was nothing in their expressions to aid him in his choice. They were leaving it up to him.

And for all his arguments and logic he knew with a terrible certainty what his decision would be. He felt it, as he felt now the reasons for their being out here at all: to seek and find and learn whatever there was to be found and learned. The ship could absorb a great deal with its automatic devices. It could store far more knowledge than could man. But there were some things the ship couldn't do. It couldn't seek out and wonder about things; and it couldn't make abstract decisions. Max Landin could.

"Secure for landing," he said softly. "We're altering course."

With the new course co-ordinates fed into the computers, the ship homed in on the beamed signal, roaring into the thin hostile atmosphere of the mass, retrorockets decelerating as it circled the mass twice before coming down on the guiding signal.

The shock of deceleration ceased. The ship came to rest; the hum of its instruments and the hiss of air conditioner units the only sounds in the cabin as they lay quietly for several minutes, gradually adjusting to the light gravity of the mass that let them unclamp and climb down and walk instead of floating in weightlessness.

It was then that they heard the tapping on the ship's hull.

They looked around, first at each other and then at the sealed port of the cabin that separated them from the air lock and the outer port of the ship. The tapping came again, loud and insistent on the outer hull. For a moment nobody moved, then Max recovered enough to switch on the ship's floodlights and step to the view-scope.

Haverson and Berger were at his elbow. "What is it?" Haverson whispered anxiously.

"Nothing," Max muttered. "Can't make out anything at all." He turned away from the scope. "See for yourselves."

The floodlights barely penetrated the absolute darkness around the ship, revealing a little barren rocky ground, and the scope couldn't be trained along the now vertical sides of the ship. And the tapping came again, louder; an eerie ringing sound that penetrated the length of the ship, playing on their nerves.

"Help me break out a suit, Will," Max said.

"You're not going out there?" Ed Haverson interrupted.

Max gave him a hard look. "What would you

suggest? Let whatever it is in here?" Certain now that only some form of intelligent life could have sent out a signal such as they had received, he didn't let himself even speculate as to what type of creature it might be. But whoever or whatever it was, it was waiting just outside the ship, and to leave without attempting contact was unthinkable.

He smiled uneasily, putting his thoughts into words, "To leave without at least shaking hands wouldn't be hospitable."

"What makes you think they're looking for hospitality?" Haverson asked quietly.

Max shrugged. "What makes you think they're not?"

He threw a switch, pressurizing the air lock, and as Will Berger helped him into a suit, the tapping came again. "Shouldn't one of us go with you?" Will suggested.

"No," Max answered thoughtfully. "If they're hostile, I don't think two of us would be any better off than one. And the ship needs its crew. Besides, it's my responsibility."

They tested the suit and the communicator in the helmet, and when the green light showed above the sealed cabin door Max nodded and Ed Haverson handed him a thermal pistol and a solar torch and opened the air-lock port.

Inside the lock the tapping on the outer hull port was louder than ever, as Max waited for the light above the cabin port to glow red when the chamber had depressurized. And when the light finally turned red it was several moments before he could bring himself to give the order over the communicator: "Open the outer port." His voice shook with suppressed excitement.

The outer port slid open and Max Landin's torch illuminated the man who was standing on the ship's ladder looking in. Suited in close-fitting glossy-smooth material, his face was clearly visible through the transparent globe that covered his head. As he raised a gloved hand to shield his eyes from the light, Max lowered his torch so that it shone on the deck of the chamber but still reflected on the alien in the open portway.

It was incredible. Except for a completely hairless face and head, the man was almost identical to themselves. And Max was suddenly aware that the alien was speaking. The voice was coming through his communicator, the sounds human but unintelligible. And then another voice, Berger's, cutting in: "Max? You all right?"

"Yes, yes, I'm all right."

"Well, what is it?"

"It's a man," Max Landin said.

The alien was talking freely now, and motioning with his arm. He had not attempted to enter the ship.

"Listen," Max spoke hurriedly, "is Ed listening to this? He's the linguist; see if he can make any of it out."

Haverson's voice came in on the communicator: "Can't read him at all, skipper. It's like nothing we've got on Earth. Does he really look human?"

"He's human," Max said. "He's motioning with his arm—I think he wants me to go with him."

Haverson's voice came back at him, "Skipper, he's got a language; I can crack it sure, break down the sound components. It'll take time."

Max had been watching the alien closely. The expression in the man's eyes was one of urgent need. "I'm afraid we don't have time, Ed," he said. "And he doesn't either. I'm going with him."

There was no answer on the communicator.

"Did you read me? Ed? Will?"

"We read you."

"I'll maintain contact," Max said. "If anything happens, reset the course co-ordinates and continue the voyage." He nodded to the alien, motioning him down; and hooking his torch and pistol on his belt, Max climbed after him through the outer port and descended awkwardly down the ship's ladder to the ground.

Activating the magnetic locator on his belt so he would be able to find his way back, he started after the alien, who was shining his own lamp on the ground ahead of him and seemed to know exactly where he was going.

As they moved in silence across the dead mass, weird-shaped rock formations rose like grotesque giants around them; and just beyond the small tight circles of their lights pressed the formless dark of perpetual night. Max, hurrying along behind the alien, felt a growing and profound respect for the whole fantastic experience.

He'd known of course that somewhere among the myriad worlds beyond the stars there had to be other intelligent races. They'd even found proof in the first expedition to Mars where archeologists had probed the ruins and canals of a civilization that was old when the Earth was still in its neolithic stage. But the chances were so slight of ever happening on other beings like themselves in anything as vast and unending as the universe—and that it should be happening to him!

"Are you reading us, skipper?" Haverson's voice came over the communicator, interrupting his thoughts.

"I read you," Max answered. "We're still moving away from the ship. Nothing to see but rocks and darkness."

But moments later the alien stopped and pointed his lamp off to the right and up on a ledge where the light illuminated the broken, mangled wreckage of a space ship, a ship almost twice the size of Max Landin's. Then the alien's lamp left the wreckage in darkness and shone ahead of him to where two more aliens in space suits waited, one of them standing, but the other lying motionless on the ground beside him.

Stunned by the sight, Max approached them cautiously, whispering into his mouthpiece. "Ed? Will? There are two more of them. And a ship; or what's left of one. They don't belong here either; they crashed."

Moving to the alien on the ground, he knelt and peered through the globe. The man's features were ashy pale and there was blood in one corner of his mouth. His eyes were closed but he was still alive, his breath coming in shallow gasps. "One of them is hurt. Hurt bad."

Rising, he looked at the other two; and the three of them, the man from Earth and the two from somewhere out beyond, stood there in their circles of brightness, staring vacantly at each other, no one seeming to know what to do next.

Max knew of course what should be done, and what the aliens expected him to do. They had crashed, and somehow these three had survived. And he saw now the instrument that had evidently been sending out the distress signal Haverson had intercepted. It was lying on the ground near the injured man, silent now that it had brought help. Only that was the tragic irony of it. There was no help he could give.

Will Berger's voice came over the communicator, and obviously the same thoughts had occurred to him: "They expect us to help them, Max."

"I know what they expect!" Max snapped. It was getting to him now, the inner turmoil of an impossible situation. Berger knew, and Haverson too, that there was nothing he could do. Nothing any of them could do. He shivered involuntarily, to think that the first contact with other beings— a chance meeting and maybe the only one they would ever have—should result in this.

"What are you going to do?" Berger's voice, tense, uncertain.

"What *can* I do?"

Silence.

Then Berger's voice again, "We can't—just leave them, can we?"

"You know the answer to that," Max's voice

was harsh with the strain of command. "The oxygen and food replenishers, all carefully calculated for six men, not nine. There's nothing we can do." But he didn't really believe that; he wouldn't let himself believe it. He knew that somehow there must be something . . .

The alien who had led him here was motioning toward himself and the others and then pointing in the direction of Max's ship. Max slowly shook his head. Then, with motions and with signs scratched on the hard ground, he tried to explain their numbers and how three more would be too many, and he seemed to be getting it across. The two aliens looked at each other and then back at the man from Earth and their eyes burned with grim horror. Then one of them knelt and scratched three lines on the ground and carefully rubbed out two of them. He pointed to the remaining line and then to the injured alien lying beside him.

Ed Haverson's voice came over the communicator, "Skipper? What's happening?"

"He wants to know if one of them can go—the injured one."

It just might be possible, Max was thinking. Maybe, by making a few fine adjustments of the instruments, a few compensations, they could take on one more man. But only one. "We might be able to compensate for one," he said. "We'd be taking a chance."

"I think we ought to try, Max," Will Berger's voice cut in.

"But shouldn't we take one of the able ones?" Haverson offered. "We'll have enough problems without the burden of an injury."

Max looked down at the alien on the ground. If there were only more time. They could find a way to communicate; find out who they were and where they came from, so many questions to remain unanswered—unless they could get one of them away alive. He didn't like the idea of taking on an injured man either, but he felt the choice was theirs. He had to give them that much.

Stooping, he scratched a single line on the ground and nodded. The aliens bent over their companion, then straightened suddenly, shock and hurt in their expressions.

Max knelt beside the injured man. There was a froth of blood on his lips, and he was no longer breathing.

Will Berger's voice came over the communicator, "Max? What's the decision?"

"The injured one is dead," Max answered.

"Then we'll take one of the others?"

"Yes," Max said, and he showed the aliens with signs and motions that one of them could still go.

But only one. A terrible choice, he knew; but what else could they do? What they did almost unnerved him.

They looked at each other, and then at the man from Earth, and they shook their heads. And kneeling slowly, they put out their lamps and bowed their heads inside their transparent globes. He could hear their voices over his communicator, murmuring softly in their strange tongue. He stared, almost unbelieving.

Will Berger's voice cut in, "Max, what's going on? Is one of them coming?"

"They're praying," said Max Landin soberly.

"They're what?"

"Praying. They're kneeling down with their heads bowed—praying."

"Oh."

And looking up at the black sky and the high, far stars, Max knew that somewhere among them was a sun and moon and the mother Earth, and God. He wondered if it was the same God; and the magnitude of the thought brought tears to his eyes as he realized for the first time the real purpose of his life in space, the meaning of it and reason for it. Now he knew what it was he had to do.

As the aliens rose and turned on their lamps and stood in their meager pools of light, enclosed by the blackness of a world alien to them all, Max made his last decision; quickly, while the courage and the dream were there. Stooping, he drew two lines on the ground and pointed at the aliens and then toward the ship, and unfastening the locator on his belt, he handed it to one of them and motioned again toward the ship.

"Skipper?" Haverson's voice on the communicator. "Have they decided?"

"They've decided," Max said. "They're coming."

"You mean both of them?"

"Listen," Max's voice was tight with emotion. "Listen closely. One of them wouldn't go without the other, and we need them. We just can't afford to lose this contact. Take them on board. Both of them."

"But, Max, that means—"

"I know what it means."

"Max, you can't do it!"

"You're wrong," Max countered. "I can't do anything else. They're on their way. Take them. That's an order."

Reaching up to his helmet, he turned off his communicator and stood there, watching the aliens' lights melt away in the blackness. Then he looked down at the dead one at his feet and a quick cold terror gripped him; for a moment he was near panic. He wanted to run after them, to cry out; but he forced himself to look again at the sky, to realize that to die was not the worst that could happen to a man.

And a strange calmness came over him. Here for the first time was something besides black voids, minerals and metals and cold dead worlds. Here was another race of men, and this way there would be time; he was giving them time to decode the alien tongue, to establish a common ground for communication, for understanding and knowledge. Switching off his torch, he stood looking up at the eternal brilliance of the farthest stars.

He no longer felt the terrible aloneness. Instead, he felt he really belonged. For the first time in his life, he really belonged in space.

QUADS FROM VARS

by William W. Greer

"Quads, we all know Vars leads space in every field. The sun fuels our ships and cities. It even fuels us. What other planet can duplicate our marvelous perfection of photosynthesis?"

President Twitch of the planet Vars lifted his starboard hand and touched his skin, which was the color and texture of poison ivy. He was addressing his Cabinet, called in special session.

"And yet," he continued, his four eyes blazing indignation, "I have it on authority of our waveless sonar auditors that lowly earthmen, our distant neighbors, boast of certain forms which we do not have."

The statement electrified the Cabinet members. They sat up straight on their stools and uncrossed their four legs. Their four trumpets—forward, aft, port, and starboard—stood out straight to catch every word.

"Yes," Twitch went on, building up his Cabinet's curiosity, "I agree it is difficult to believe earthman can offer us anything. He is a creature untold centuries behind us. Earthman actually is designed to see, speak, walk, hear, and smell in one direction only. He would be amazed to see our all-purpose trumpets, through which we speak, hear, and smell, and which furl when not in use. He might even be alarmed to see our four eyes, also spaced equally about our heads, for seeing in any direction. He could not believe that we also have four legs, which permit us to move with equal speed in any direction; likewise our four hands, so necessary in this modern day of gadgets, controls, and automation."

Twitch, standing on the centrum, surrounded by a veritable field of eager green trumpets, enjoyed the fixed attention. "We take for granted so many of our developments," he said. "Our photosynthesis, for example. Would you believe that earthman still stokes his body with great quantities of bulk through an opening in his face called a mouth? He fuels at least three times a day, whereas a few effortless hours in the sun each week, plus an occasional mineral bath, suffice us."

Now Twitch seemingly changed the subject. "Fellow quads," he said, "the holiday season is approaching, the time of the year so dear to all quadlets. Can we deny them anything? Yet I have here a report from our monitors, who daily tap earth's radio, which indicates that earthmen delight their young, called children, with institutions called zoos."

Twitch saw the puzzled expression around him, and explained: "In our zeal for advancement, we long ago eliminated all forms of lower life. Our scientists say all flora vanished from Vars ten thousand years ago, when we extended the hard-surfaced travel plain to cover the entire planet. Earthman, oddly enough, maintains a primitive form of life which he refers to as animals. He harbors them in structures and parks he calls zoological gardens. Children by the thousands visit these areas in never-ending fascination. Quads, we simply must have animals, if we would continue to pride ourselves as the leaders of space."

Birthbath, the Secretary of Space, leaped to his four feet and posed a question: "Mr. President, following your colorful description, it occurs to me that our quadlets might find greater amusement in earthman himself, than in these creatures you call animals. It's utterly amazing!"

"A good point, Birthbath. I've considered just that, but ruled it out, at least for a few centuries. Earthman is dangerous, despite his retarded civilization. For example, our space glasses show earth literally crawling with microscopic forms. Contrary to some beliefs, these forms are not man himself, but what he calls automobiles. In these travel-units, obviously under no central control, earthman becomes alarmingly destructive, by sheer force of numbers. We must learn more about man and his weapons before we attempt to seize him. Besides, earthman lives very poorly in captivity."

Bulgout, the Secretary of Atmosphere, raised his port and starboard hands.

"Yes, Bulgie?"

"Mr. President, how do you propose to get these animals? Steal them?"

"Nonsense, Bulgie." Twitch looked down his aft trumpet at the ponderous, somewhat fatuous Bulgout. "The forests of earth are full of them, free for the taking. Why should we risk man's wrath with a raid on his zoos? All of which leads me to the details of Operation Animal."

Twitch stepped from the centrum, walked to a wall and touched a button with a finger of his aft hand. A huge globe of the earth lowered from the ceiling. Using a pointer held in his port hand,

Twitch said: "Here's the area we'll visit. It's the great Calaskan Forest, home of many animals . . ."

"Pardon me, Mr. President," interrupted Knott, the Secretary of Planetary Travel, "but who is we?"

"We is we," said Twitch, "and I mean just that. You, and you, and you and you . . . any of my Cabinet members who will volunteer . . . and I myself will lead the expedition!"

The room was suddenly a bed of agitated trumpets, like flowers bending and bobbing in a high wind, all blaring at once. "Twitch? Twitch himself . . . Twitch himself . . . will you go? and you? . . . We'll ALL volunteer! . . ."

Around the planet, mingled emotions greeted news of the expedition. Some gossipers labeled it a political move on Twitch's part, since he had already announced his candidacy for a fourth term and another one hundred and fifty years in office. The success of Operation Animal would cinch his election. Yet, withal, the planet stood behind Twitch in this magnificent venture. "A great quad, that Twitch, he'll go down in universal history," they said. A few felt that the great leader should not risk his life on such a hazardous project. But Twitch was adamant. Plans formulated rapidly.

The gigantic sphere-ship stood ready for take-off. By special arrangement, the expeditionary vehicle was fixed by magnetic beams to the planet Coldfire, only a million light years away. The departure would be simply a matter of swinging out into space on these beams, as an acrobat swings on his trapeze. At the proper moment the beams would be broken, and the ship would swoop in a great arc toward earth, just as the acrobat zips through space to bounce into a net.

Twitch raised his four hands in a final farewell to the thousands of quads, quaddles, and quadlets assembled on the runway below him. They shifted about like tall crabs, seeking a better view of their illustrious leader.

Twitch paused for a moment to smile on the multitude and enjoy the adoration. Then he suddenly gave his pilots the signal. Slowly the great sphere moved tractionless along the space travel field, then accelerated like a mighty pendulum. Faster and faster it swung into the cloudless sky. Within seconds it was lost to the view of the quads of Vars.

Twitch sat with the controllers until the beams with Coldfire were cut and the solar-receivers began to hum. Then he wavelessed Vars that all was well and retired midship to join his Cabinet.

"Gentlequads," he said, "I'm hungry. Anybody care to join me in the solarium for a snack?"

Bulgout was the first to speak. "I'm with you," he said. Bulgie was known for his appetite. He could never get enough sun. He was always the last to leave the solestaurants, and his green skin was a little parched.

As the sphere swung through space, a miniature planet in itself, Twitch discussed the earth venture. "We know very little about these things called animals," he said, "just scraps of intelligence picked up now and then by waveless. We do know that they vary greatly in size, appearance, and behavior. But we do not know how they will greet us, or how to converse with them. We will learn much. We must feel our way into this project, play it by trumpet, so to speak."

Within hours the ship's navigators picked up earth on the kinematic screen. The pilots, only too aware of the historical significance of the trip and the importance of the passengers, had maintained the solar-receiver at top rev. The huge sphere had performed beautifully. But now, with earth in sight only a few hundred miles away, the ship circled for hours, waiting for the proper juxtaposition of earth and sun which would cast the great night shadow upon the Calaskan Forest.

"It's all right," said Twitch to his Cabinet members, who now had butterflies deep inside

them somewhere in the area of their midriffs.
"We're storing away excess fuel which we'll need
when we ride the night-beam in. We make contact
at midnight, the hour of sleep for western earth."

Through the sphere-ship's vast picture windows
the top brass of Vars could see the gloom of night
crawl across the face of the tiny earthball. Twitch
was now in the control dome, peering through
space glasses and giving orders to pilots and navigators. Slowly the space ship's speed reduced as it
placed earth between itself and the sun.

"That's the spot," Twitch said, "bring us in
there, under cover of darkness." The pilots cut the
solar-receivers and throttled the antigravitational
rotars. Now earth loomed tremendous before
them as night closed in, darker and darker.

A mile above the great slumbering forest the
operators opened wide the rotar throttles and all
aboard could feel the gentle but powerful braking
which thrust them forward in their seats. The
ship slowed to a float, then drifted gently in, its
great light beams fingering the tree tops.

"There," said Twitch, "make magnetic contact with that tall green monument—er—that
tree by the small body of water."

The pilots maneuvered their million-ton ship
deftly. The split second it touched the tip of the
poplar tree by the lake, they advanced the anti-

gravitational throttles the merest fraction of a centimeter, fixed the magnetic contact needle on dead center, and cut all other switches. The sphere-ship rested gently in the uppermost branches of the tree, as snug as a ball on the tip of a juggler's finger.

"Beautifully done," said Twitch. "Beautiful." He patted the crew on the back, four at a time.

"My feet are killing me," whined Bulgout. He was sitting on his bunk midship soaking his four feet in a moist, specially-prepared mixture of synthetic dirt, sand, and pebbles. He always carried a carton of the expensive foot-mix on long trips. His feet seemed to need it. They soaked it up and gave him greater strength.

All day the Cabinet officers had prowled about through the deep, gloomy forest. It is true they had found the towering trees and dense undergrowth amazing and delightful. But the urgency of their animal-hunting mission had not permitted full enjoyment of this strange new world. They were constantly on the search for something called an animal, yet all they could find was themselves, in the most unexpected spots. They'd hear a noise, and scurry in pursuit about the base of some giant tree, only to bump trumpets with another officer, also pursuing the sound. Now they were gathered despondently back on the ship, their emerald skins scratched by briers, their multiple shins bruised by fallen logs. Several were beginning to think the trip was a mistake.

"How can we catch an animal," asked Knott, "if we don't even know what an animal looks like?"

"Please, gentlequads," said Twitch. "It takes time. I'm sure we'll fare better tomorrow. Just remember, animals have four feet, just like us. Now let's get a little sleep." But Twitch was the only one who didn't sleep. Late into the night he read and re-read all the reports available on earth-zoos and the creatures in them. But he couldn't find much that helped.

It was Twitch, however, who found the first animal. He saw it the next day shuffling quietly under the trees, and called to it. The creature stopped and Twitch studied it carefully, then consulted the sheaf of papers he carried in his built-in pouch. He saw nothing that described this creature, but he did remember a sentence he'd read last night. "Some animals," it had said, "camouflage or disguise themselves, so that they blend into the background of their habitat, especially when frightened or in danger . . . "

Twitch scrutinized the creature again. It looked considerably like one of the hassocks, the clumps of stiff grass, he had seen near the lakeshore.

"But you can't fool me," Twitch said softly, "I saw you move." He walked closer, and saw the stems of coarse grass rise. "And there's no wind," Twitch thought. "Come, animal," he said, "I am a friend, and will give you a good home."

The animal did not respond. "Shy," thought Twitch, and quickly stooped to grasp it in his arms. But he arose with a harsh cry of anguish, his dark green skin resembling a pin cushion, pierced by a dozen or more sharp quills.

Twitch painfully plucked the barbs away, his trumpets moaning softly. Then, as he hurried toward the ship for first aid, he forgot his pain as he heard a strange commotion. Bursting through the foliage near the lake, he beheld a scene which stopped the sap in his veins. The mammoth ship lay partially submerged, half filling the lake. Angry waters were surging down the once-placid brook. His Cabinet members and the crew were jabbering excitedly.

"Holy Sunfire," Twitch cried, "What happened?"

"The tree collapsed and the ship sank into the

water," said Birdbath. "Now we are in a quizzle!"

"But there was no pressure on that tree," Twitch said, "not more than the fraction of an ounce. We used it as the negative pole for our anti-gravity magnetic contact."

Twitch waded out through the rushing water to the stump of the poplar and examined it closely. "Just as I thought," he said. "This tree didn't break. It was deliberately cut. We've been sabotaged."

Everyone gathered about the stump. "I'll be jiggered," exclaimed Bulgout, "you're right!" The pointed stump bore the long smooth incisions of an extremely sharp cutting instrument.

They were all so excited they did not see the furry creature which surfaced nearby in the lake. Its small intelligent eyes took one look at the weird scene on shore, then its tail spanked the water with a loud clap and it disappeared.

Everybody jumped and Twitch cried: "What was that?"

Every trumpet unfurled and stood out like a bugle sounding reveille, but detected no sound, no scent. Then from Twitch's trumpets came the orders, clear, sharp, and definite.

"Quads," he blared, "I declare vartial law. The ship will no longer be left unguarded. Pilots, enter the control dome, center the ship and lift it to the tip of yonder tallest tree, then remain at your posts, making any repairs necessary."

Addressing his Cabinet, Twitch continued: "We shall not return empty-handed. We must find an animal. Go again into the forest, and let no quad idle!"

"YESSIR," they said, and shuffled off into the somber forest.

Surprisingly enough, it was Bulgout who found an animal. He saw it walking pigeon-toed and funny through the trees. Stifling an outburst, Bulgie said: "Your feet must hurt just like mine. Say, you're pretty, aren't you?" Bulgie admired the white stripes and the bushy tail. "Come on, now. Let us shake hands and be friends."

The plump Cabinet officer advanced slowly and saw the bushy tail salute him. "Ah, the sign of friendship," he observed, confusing aft and forward extremities, "but why don't you speak?" Bulgie drew nearer and the tail became more erect. "You do like me, don't you, whether you say hello or not?"

Carefully and rather timidly Bulgie reached down with his port, starboard, and forward hands and shook hands with the lovely tail.

"Oh my!" he said, "but you carry a strong aroma." Bulgie's skin turned flesh-colored with a

slight nausea as he gathered the animal close to him. "But we shall bathe you and you shall be our first zoo." Bulgie was not yet too clear about the difference between zoo and animal.

"I hope I shan't be ill," Bulgie thought as he hurried to the lake, clutching the creature tightly. "Now to give you a good cleansing," he addressed the animal, "before Twitch and the rest return. I just hope they don't find anything. Think of old Bulgout, a hero. They'll pop their trumpets when they see what I've got."

Again and again Bulgie dunked the squirming creature in the cold water, then sprayed him with a combination aphis killer and fungicide which he always carried in his pouch. But the animal did not respond to the type of ablution so soothing and purifying to the chlorophyl-loaded quads. Its pungence became overpowering. Finally, with a cry of distress, Bulgout dropped the creature into the water, clapped his four hands over his four wilted trumpets, and rushed blindly into the forest.

Bulgout hurled himself into the soft, sweet-smelling loam and rolled like a log. He stretched and rooted his limbs deep into the cleansing soil, feeling it cool and moist against his hot skin. And then, as he wallowed in the primeval mold, he experienced a strangely atavistic, delightful sensation. It was like a haunting, long-lost melody, velvet-smooth and evasive, which slipped past Bulgie's senses as through a net, leaving a blank emotion. He lay there for a long time.

The great sphere-ship zoomed through space, returning to Vars with not a single animal aboard. But there was no gloom, no depression among the Cabinet officers and their leader. They were lounging in the solarium in an atmosphere of gayety and occasional hilarity. Their feet were firmly planted in deep containers filled with the rich earth-soil. The animated conversation buzzing among them stopped as Twitch cleared his trumpets and gestured for attention. All the Cabinet members turned toward their peerless leader.

"Quads," he said, reaching for a handful of the earth at his feet, "I propose a toast to Bulgout, the one who has turned failure to historical success." Twitch rubbed a bit of the soil onto his gnarled old legs, and his officers responded in the toast. "It is true we did not discover that for which we came. But, thanks to Bulgout, we return with something infinitely better, an elixir of incredible restorative powers. It was Bulgout who, quite by accident and with some discomfort, discovered the miraculous, strength-building, strangely exhilarating qualities of the earth-soil. Our ship is laden with it, and I trust our scientist can break it down to its basic components and prepare more.

"It is," Twitch said with great feeling, "the greatest thing that has happened to Vars since our remote ancestors, billions of years ago, uprooted themselves and began to walk about." With a twinkle of a green tear in his eye, Twitch then said, "Bulgout, we salute you!"

Four-handed applause thundered through the solarium and all eyes turned to Bulgout, who was sitting somewhat removed from the others because of his lingering redolence. Bulgie, beaming and quite embarrassed, arose and took a bow. Then he lifted his four arms, seeking silence. The sunshine glinted on his upraised hands, flower-like trumpets, and green skin. With his stumpy legs planted in the container of soil and his sturdy trunk rising to his four outstretched arms, one could say that Bulgie very closely resembled one of the trees back in the earthman's great Calaskan Forest.